FRANCIS X

The Lethal Revenge of an
Irish American Terrorist.

F.J. Doherty with Sean Doherty

authorHOUSE®

AuthorHouse™
1663 Liberty Drive
Bloomington, IN 47403
www.authorhouse.com
Phone: 1-800-839-8640

First published by AuthorHouse 5/19/2011

ISBN: 978-1-4567-6010-6 (e)
ISBN: 978-1-4567-6011-3 (hc)
ISBN: 978-1-4567-6012-0 (sc)

Library of Congress Control Number: 2011908043

Printed in the United States of America

Prologue

"The Troubles" was a term used to describe the violence in Northern Ireland. In 1923, the country was divided and Northern Ireland became part of the United Kingdom. The rest of the country became an independent republic.

As the years past, the predominantly Roman Catholic nationalist and the Protestant unionists were openly fighting in the north. The British Army was ordered to deploy to Northern Ireland in the role of peace keepers. There were many skirmishes between the soldiers with both Protestant and the Catholics,and many died.

On January 30, 1972, a civil rights march was planned by various Catholic groups in the City of Derry that escalated into events that forever mark that day as "Bloody Sunday." Fourteen died and thirteen were wounded. All were found to be unarmed and some were shot in the back.

It remains to be known what the actual cause and motivation was that cost the lives of those Northern Ireland residents on that tragic Bloody Sunday. Many have speculated, but few have concluded. True, it was political differences fueled by religious oppression, but those are simply the facts. What is not known is the origin of the hatred that was in the hearts of those men. Whether it was the bloodlust that empowered them to think that what they were doing was for the right cause, or that they believed there was a "good" or "bad" side.

One thing was certain...what was done could never be erased. There would be no amount of apology or repentance that could cure the pain in the hearts of the Irish people. For the Irish people are a people of proud tradition. They are the ancestors of abused slaves, the children of oppressed farmers, and the fathers of revenged. This account is not simply of one person, one family, or one life. It is a mere glimpse into the mind of a people who find joy at funerals, who mourn separation, and who find solace in retribution. It is also for those people who had their lives taken on January 30, 1972 on that "Bloody Sunday."

Jack Duddy - Age 17
Paddy Doherty - Age 31
Bernard McGuigan - Age 41
Hugh Gilmore - Age 17
Kevin McElhinney - Age 17
Michael McDaid - Age 20
William Nash - Age 19
John Young - Age 17
Michael Kelly- Age 17
Jim Wray - Age 22
Gerard Donaghy - Age 17
Gerard McKinney - Age 35
William McKinney - Age 26
John Johnson - Age 59

This story is not just for them, for they will always be immortalized in the hearts, in the minds, and in the walls of Derry. This story is for you,wherever you are.

Please, do not think that freedom is a right. It is a gift. A gift that can be easily be taken away, especially if we do not understand and appreciate what it takes to achieve it. It is then and only then, that we can begin to realize the emotions of those who have fallen, those who have been wronged, and those who seek revenge.

After thirty-eight years of inquiries and investigation, the British government released an official report on June 16, 2010 that laid full responsibility on the British soldiers for the 1972 "Bloody Sunday" killings in Northern Ireland. The Prime Minister of the United Kingdom, David Cameron, announced the finding which was that the British Army had fired with no justification, and he apologized on behalf of the government and country as a whole.

"It can be proclaimed to the world that the civil rights marchers of 'Bloody Sunday' were innocent, one and all," said Tony Doherty, the son of one of those killed.

What you have just read is fact. What you are about to read is a combination of both fact and fiction. You can decide where to draw the line.

"Do it to them before they do it to you."
-FX's Golden Rule-

Chapter 1

The odious stench of gunpowder still loomed in the air near Derry, Ireland. The street cleaners had their work cut out for them, still attempting to erase the crimson tears off the street from the events of the weeks past. It was a mere fourteen days after the "Bogside Massacre" and life in Derry was still and silent.

Commerce was thriving at the norm. The schools and government offices were back to their daily routines. Now everything was tainted; life was tainted. As such the way in Ireland, however, citizens took to the pubs to seek refuge. Even in the midst of the troubles, a "pour house" was seen as almost as important as a house of worship. As the glasses were filled, the bar keeps would listen to the Irish people talk about the pain and sadness that riddled their hearts through their muddled accents.

In a pub on Strand Road, frequented by British soldiers and North of Ireland loyalists, a different conversation was taking place.

"Shall we raise our glasses?" the first soldier said.

"Whatever for?" a second soldier asked.

"For the clean-up of Northern Ireland," the first soldier replied.

"Ah yes! Of course it's for the clean-up of this God forsaken place. We will help make it one of the cleanest countries on earth by putting the scum in the ground or in a British prison," shouted the second soldier.

At that point, the bar keep came over and inquired as to why the men were celebrating in such a time of mourning. The four soldiers explained that the trash was being removed from the country and it was only fitting they celebrate. One of the soldiers raised his glass and made a toast.

"Cheers to a bloody Sunday. No, rather, cheers to a bloody GOOD Sunday!"

The men proceeded to buy rounds for all the patrons in the bar.

Chapter 2

The rigid steel door latched with a bang. The nights at Danbury Connecticut Federal Prison were cold and tedious, but had become the norm for Bernard O'Donnell or "Barney" to his friends. Bernard was a full time construction worker and part time terrorist whose run-ins with the law had been frequent and violent before escaping to the always welcoming Ellis Island in New York to begin a new life for his family.

Barney was wanted by Great Britain for a myriad of criminal offenses, including bombings, arson and violence against British soldiers; however to the people who lived near him in Boston, he was a sweet and affectionate worker who seemed to solely live for his wife and two children, both of whom were born in the United States.

In 1981, he was apprehended and taken to Danbury Prison where he awaited his deportation date.

The night before his departure, he knelt down by his cot and prayed.

"Dear Lord, I do ask that you watch over my children and wife. I know that I will see them someday and they will be strong for me while I am gone, I love them with all my heart."

Barney started to get up, but as he did another thought started forming in his head. He put his hands together and looked up in the sky at the divine power watching over him and said in a calm Irish whisper, "and Lord, I ask for forgiveness for the sins I have committed, but I regret none of them."

And with that, Barney left the United States on a plane back to Belfast. He was going to be left in the North of Ireland for seven days while authorities attempted to find a suitable long term holding facility that Barney was going to need for the remainder of his days.

The Brown Stone Jail on the outskirts of Belfast was the highest level of security and for only the most vicious of criminals. It was here that Bernard O'Donnell arrived on a brisk Monday night.

The day's events in the jail were monotonous. Prisoners were fed and enjoyed some recreational activities and visits from family and friends. The commissioner in charge noticed that one prisoner was absent from the dining hall.

"Rogers. Where is prisoner number 144146?" he asked sternly. "Sir, he was moved to solitary confinement last night. The warden in charge thought he was too much of a risk to have around the other prisoners."

"Well bring him some food will you? Can't have the man looking abused when Scotland Yard arrives."

With that, Rogers went into the solitary confinement wing of the jail and with a rattle of his keys he unlocked the large door, only to find Bernard O'Donnell dead. The guard immediately vomited from the ghastly sight. Barney was sitting up in his bed with a twelve inch butcher knife protruding from his throat. Through the pools of blood that cascaded on the floor, Rogers bent down to discover a note that was attached to the end of the blade.

The note read, "Thank you America for sending him back. We have been his judge, his jury, and his executioner. God save the queen."

Authorities were quick to cover up this potentially high profile murder. With the aid of Scotland Yard and the American Ambassador, the cause of death was unquestionably ruled a suicide.

The jail and county still felt the need to issue a statement to calm the questioning minds of the Irish people. Too much speculation could be disastrous.

"Whether or not Mr. O'Donnell had been murdered was never brought into question," the commissioner said in a statement that he released. "It was simply a suicide of a very depressed man with a history of physical violence. The only people that had been allowed into Mr. O'Donnell's chamber, the night of the suicide, were the prison guards, Timothy Moore, Thomas Livingston, and their supervisor, British Army Sergeant Phillip Johnson. After an official inquiry, his death was officially listed as a suicide."

Upon hearing of the news of her husband's death, O'Donnell's wife flew back to Ireland to start making the necessary arrangements. As she sat on the plane, her vale adorned in black and her heart broken with sorrow, she could not believe that Barney's death was a suicide. Her gut told her that he had to have fallen victim to violence. They had been through so much together in their life; she knew he was a strong man who had overcome many hardships and would not be the one to bring his own life to an end. It just didn't make any sense.

Once in Ireland, she made sure that her husband received the proper burial outside of their farm which was just south of Cranford in County Donegal. Barney was finally home.

Chapter 3

As he strolled through Boston's North End, Francis Xavier O'Donnell spotted a shiny penny glistening in the summer sun. Never one to pass up a bit of extra luck, Francis took the penny and placed it in his right front pocket. Not that Francis needed a whole lot of extra luck these days. He was an extremely successful entrepreneur with an undergraduate degree from Boston College in bio chemical engineering and a graduate degree from Massachusetts Institute of Technology (M.I.T.) to soften the blow if his business ventures were to fail.

Francis was a strikingly handsome man, standing about six feet tall, with course, dark and shiny hair like that of some wayward Asian ancestor. His eyes were as black as coal and his heart and soul were equally as dark. He was not only a scholar, but also a soldier.

While attending Boston College, Francis enrolled in the Reserve Officers' Training Corps (ROTC) program to help defray the cost of his tuition. Francis became drawn to the action and excitement of the Green Berets.

After two tours in Iraq as a U.S. Army Green Beret, Francis received two Purple Hearts and a Silver Star (the Army's 3rd highest award for valor).

When asked about his commendations, Francis would simply reply, "The Purple Heart I got because I forgot to duck. The Silver Star was given to a bunch of people."

While serving in Iraq as a Special Forces Captain, Francis and two sergeants were detailed to pick up a terrorist from the Iraqi police, who had planted a road side bomb that killed one U.S. Marine and wounded three others. When they brought the prisoner back to the U.S. authorities, someone noticed a bruise on the prisoner's cheek which launched an investigation into the possible abuse of the prisoner by Francis and his sergeants. Francis made it known to the investigators that all Al-Qaeda terrorists have a book of instructions on what to say and do if they are captured. The very first rule in the book is to immediately claim that you were abused by your captors.

Regardless of Francis's claims, the investigation persisted and lasted eight months. During that time, Francis and his men were treated like criminals.

All the charges were eventually dismissed; however, it left a very bitter taste in Francis' mouth, one that would take a case of mouth wash to get rid of. That was the point when Francis thought of his own country as his enemy and he chose to end his military career.

Francis received an honorable discharge as well as a one hundred percent disability which was awarded due to his wounds. Francis believed that although he would never consider himself connected to America, he was proud to fight for the country, but prouder to fight for himself.

Francis X used the money that he received from his discharge to begin his very lucrative and innovative company, Irish Shopping Ltd. This was an all-inclusive tour service, which afforded the opportunity to Irish citizens to visit America and shop for three days to their hearts content. The strong Euro was a great incentive and business was thriving.

"Give them what they want," Francis would tell his employees.

The business was so successful that Francis was able to open up several locations in Dublin, Galway, Cork, and Donegal, with the home office in Boston.

With the fruits of his labor, Francis was able to purchase a condominium on the Boston waterfront as well as a country home in Ireland in the small coastal town of Dalkey, which was on the outskirts of Dublin.

In addition to being a great businessman, Francis was loved by all those who knew him. He was especially admired for his loyalty to family and friends. However, Francis trusted no one. Everyone inside his inner circle was known as "The Cousins," and it was with them and only them that Francis trusted with his life.

Chapter 4

One warm summer night, Francis was sitting with two of "The Cousins," Paul Donovan and Bill Hanlon on his patio overlooking Boston Harbor and the Logan Airport. As the planes landed and departed, they watched the moon glisten over the water. It was a perfect evening.

Visitors to Boston are always amazed at the beauty of the Boston waterfront and of the Boston Harbor Islands. A lot of the islands have a visitor center and a wealth of history. There are one thousand and sixty acres and thirty-six miles of undeveloped shoreline on the Harbor Islands.

The harbor also has the Boston Harbor Walk where one can walk from the Italian North End to the Irish South Boston. Ships of every size and shape can be seen crisscrossing in the harbor. The airport is also located on the harbor, which adds to the ever moving and ever changing beauty of one of the greatest tourist cities in the country. Boston is also home to the oldest commissioned ship in the U.S. Navy the USS Constitution (Old Ironsides), which was built in Boston in 1787. The ship is a premier tourist attraction at the harbor.

****

Paul poured Francis another vodka martini, which was Francis' favorite drink, despite the misnomer that all Irish men drank whiskey or beer. Bill looked to Francis and asked, "What seems to be the problem?"

Francis responded in harsh mixed tone of a Boston accent and a southern Irish brogue, "I'm just sitting here thinking about my father."

"Your father?" Bill replied.

"Indeed. It's a shame he couldn't be here today to see what I have done for the O'Donnell name."

"You have done your old man well there Francis. I'm sure he would be proud of you. Let's raise a glass to Barney O'Donnell!" Paul said gleefully.

"I have a better idea," Francis said. His voice became stern and soft. "I think it's time we take care of the three fuckers that murdered my father."

"You are a mad bastard Francis, you know that?! How are we to do that?" Paul asked.

"Don't worry gentleman," Francis said while he raised his glass. "I have a plan."

Chapter 5

In Ballymena, just outside of Derry, an old man by the name of Tom Livingston was spending a quiet evening at home. Since his retirement from the Northern Ireland corrections department, Livingston had become solemn and grumpy while living off of his pension. He was a wretched old man that wouldn't find happiness on Christmas morning and whose shrewd and uninviting attitude warranted for little return care from his community. On that night, Livingston was settling down to watch "Coronation Street" with a microwaveable meal from the local shop. Just as he sat down, the doorbell rang.

"Aw for fuck's sake, leave me be."

Again, the doorbell rang.

"Jesus Christ, you stupid bastards, go away!"

A voice from the other side of the door beckoned, "Please sir, me and my mate broke down up the road. Would you please let us use your phone?"

"The fuck I will. Try the petrol station down the way you lousy fuck."

"Please sir, my friend is quite ill."

Livingston ignored the plea. The bell began to ring incessantly. As Livingston got up, he could not help but wonder if perhaps it was a real emergency of some sort. Of course, he ultimately couldn't care less. He approached the door and opened it hastily.

"What the fu---!"

As soon as the door opened, Livingston was bashed in the head with a small pipe, instantly knocking him backwards and two men barged into his home. They forced him into a chair in his dining room. The men, both in black masks, did their best to cause as much harm to Livingston without rendering him unconscious. After they tied him, they began their inquisition.

"Tell us what you know about Barney O'Donnell's murder!" one of the masked man barked.

"You lousy fuckin' bastards. I'll be telling you shit!"

The second man then punched him square in the jaw.

"I'll ask ye again, you faggot, tell us what you know about the murder," he said in a cold whisper.

Angered, Livingston spit in the man's face. "Fuck off! I didn't see shit!"

At that point, the second man pulled out a .22 caliber gun and immediately shot Livingston in the foot. Livingston began to scream as blood seeped from the fresh wound.

"Now the next time it'll be yer knee," the first man said. "Tell us about the murder."

Livingston began to cave. "OK, OK! I'll tell ye! It was Sergeant Johnson. He told me and Moore to follow his orders if we wanted to get paid. During lockdown, we went into O'Donnell's cell and held him down. Moore took his arms, and I made him kneel on his knees. But it was Sergeant Johnson who drove the knife through his throat. We didn't know he was going to do it! We thought he was just going to rough him up a bit!"

"Really?" the second man questioned. "I imagine you didn't do this as an act of charity? No offense old man, but you don't strike me as the generous type. You wouldn't even let two helpless men use your phone," he chuckled.

Frantic to give the men answers, Livingston replied, "No! We were paid well. Johnson made sure of it."

The men nodded at each other and pleased with the information, proceeded to get up, leaving Livingston tied up and bleeding in his chair. Just as they were approaching the door, the first man turned around.

"Tell me sir, why did you tell us in the beginning that you didn't see anything?"

Quivering in pain, Livingston retorted, "I don't know. I'm sorry. I don't know why."

"Well I think I have a good idea, you seem to only have two eyes. Maybe if you had a third, you'd be able to see things better." And with that, the man fired one shot clean through the forehead of Thomas Livingston, killing him instantly.

The two men departed and drove off towards Derry. Once the car was started, the second man turned to the first and said, "Third eye! Fuckin'class!"

The two laughed and drove off into the night.

Chapter 6

"We'll see you tomorrow Mr. O'Donnell," the cheerful receptionist said with a smile.

Francis gave a smile and a quick wave as he exited the M.I.T. lab towards the "T" station (Boston's transit system). Francis knew his smile could melt hearts and hide hatred better than any lie a man could tell a woman.

As he reached the "T" stop, Francis reached into his pocket and tightly held his prize. It was a long time in the making, but on this day he felt the pride of a new parent as he boarded the "T" back to the Boston waterfront.

Francis had attended M.I.T. on the military's G.I. Bill for two years, at which time he had developed his "special project." He thought, what a great country America was to pay him to make something that will someday be used against them.

Francis made a few phone calls and soon his house was in a buzz with his closest comrades, who were enjoying canapés and sipping libations with no knowledge of why this impromptu celebration was being held. But who were they to deny the invitation? Francis retreated to the balcony with two of his closest "Cousins."

"Shall we go for a quick ride up north?" Francis asked.

"To where? New Hampshire?" Meagan Fitzgerald retorted. "Why the fuck would we go up there?"

Francis laughed and said, "Let's just say the professor is taking his students on a field trip."

With that, Francis and a car full of bewildered and excited "Cousins" drove up into the White Mountain region of the Granite State. They traveled down a winding road with Francis guiding every move as though he had been there just the day before.

They reached a small farm house with an abandoned school bus parked in front of it. The "Cousins" were still confused, but excited nonetheless. What brought them to such a remote destination? Francis was about to answer their questions well beyond their expectations.

"What do you suppose this is?" Francis asked as he pulled out a small vial of clear liquid from his coat pocket.

"I hope to Christ its pocheen for dragging us this far out!" someone exclaimed. The small group laughed.

"Indeed, whilst this is not moonshine, it is in fact another Irish creation that is sure to change the world," Francis replied. "Why don't I show you."

Francis took the small vial of clear liquid that had a consistency similar to that of nail polish and splashed a bit of it on the bus. He then took a match from his coat pocket and struck it against his hat.

Meagan gasped, "Jesus! Don't be lighting matches near that. You could blow us back to Kinsale."

"Calm down dear," Francis calmly replied. "Watch."

He then placed the match to the liquid on the bus; however, nothing happened. In fact, the liquid on the bus put his match out.

"Perfect," Scott Bruce said with a snare tone. "I swear I didn't learn that water put out fire in the second grade there Francis."

"If everyone is going to be sarcastic, I have no problem ending the demonstration now. But I assure you that if your time is as valuable to you, as mine is to me, then you will not be sorry," Francis said. "Now, everyone get back into the van."

They all got back into the van and drove a quarter mile down the road when suddenly Francis stopped the van and took two small cell phones from his bag.

"What's with the phone's there?" Meagan quipped. "Who are you calling? Everyone you know is in this friggin' van."

"No Meagan, I need two to call all your ex-boyfriends. Now would you all kindly be quiet so I can explain. These are actually not cell phones. They are devices that emit radio waves. The one in my right hand is ultra low frequency device. The one in my left hand is an ultra high frequency device."

"So, if one is high and one is low, won't they just cancel each other out?" Chuck Hogarty asked.

Francis smirked. "Well, not really." He then proceeded to push the two buttons down at the same time.

The explosion sounding like a demolition of a city block suddenly erupted from the forest. Outside of the window all that the "Cousins" could see was fire and smoke.

"Let's get out of here!" Meagan yelled.

Francis started the van and as he was about to pull away a sign from the remains of the school bus landed on the hood of his vehicle. It read, "Please watch for children."

Francis laughed to himself on the ride back to Boston. He explained that it had taken him two years at M.I.T. and a lot of trial and error for the development of this explosive. His peers at M.I.T. thought he was working toward something that would improve the excavation of coal in strip mining operations; to decrease the impact on the environment. Francis told "The Cousins" that through his research and development he was able to ignite his explosive with radio waves, in a direct line of sight, for up to five thousand yards away.

Once back at Francis's condo, "The Cousins" were dumbstruck. What did they just witness? It was like an invention from some mad scientist.

"I hope you realize that this is the beginning of the end for some people, and I need your devout loyalty and trust in the months to follow. Now, I will only ask you this once. Are you with me?"

Everyone in the room nodded simultaneously in agreement.

"Good...don't worry about a thing," Francis said. "I have a plan."

Chapter 7

It was only a week after the violent killing of Tom Livingston when, in a small pub in the heart of downtown Belfast, Timothy Moore finished his nightcap. Revered by his community, Moore was a man of the people. He was a sensitive soul with a large brood and the father of Portrush selectman Seamus Moore, who was well on his way to being elected mayor.

Timothy had seven children and thirteen grandchildren. He always found time to stop by Foster's pub for a drink on his way home from his part-time job as a security guard at Belfast International Airport. A job granted to him largely in part because of his son's position but, nonetheless, he was still respected for his qualifications.

While Moore was a relatively jovial individual, he had let his appearance and physical health decline greatly. He was overweight, balding, and cared little for the growing concerns of his family. Moore was quite content with the fact that he was brought to this earth to enjoy it and to live life to the fullest. He never lived his life with any regrets, aside from perhaps one. This one regret allowed him to gain the compensation to afford the status and privilege that ultimately led to his son's position.

On that particular night, the bartender poured Moore one last

Stella then flashed the lights for last call. Moore would always be there to the very end during the work week. This schedule made Moore predicable to his wife, his children, and unbeknownst to him, his enemies. Although Moore's son propositioned for harsher punishments for drunk drivers, his father was one of the biggest offenders.

Timothy exited Foster's with a breath that could ignite the Olympic Torch. As he stumbled to his Fiat, he faintly heard footsteps behind him. He only assumed it was the harlot Sheila simply playing her dirty tricks on him once again. As he turned around, however, two people forcefully came out from the shadows and attempted to grab Moore. Realizing his danger, he attempted to run up the narrow vacant street. His vices soon got the best of him and shortly thereafter, Moore fell.

The two people then held Moore up against his car and inquired, "When the investigators asked you if you heard anything the night of Barney O'Donnell's death, you said no. What is with that?"

"I swear I didn't hear anything!" Moore said, trying to catch his breath.

"But you did hear Sergeant Johnson when he said you would be paid handsomely for your services that night. Did you not?"

Moore began to heave. The two dropped him to the ground and the fat man lay there exhausted and scared.

"Well there is apparently a good reason you didn't hear anything the night Barney was killed. You didn't have a third ear."

The bullet passed through Timothy Moore's head and his panting and wheezing ceased.

"Two down, one to go," Kathleen said.

Chapter 8

"Fucking Fahmahs!" the drunk college girl yelled as she was escorted out the door by two security guards. "Paddy bastids."

It was just another night in the Brighton section of Boston, where the nineteen year olds with their sister's driver's licenses in hand thought they were invincible when it came to doing shots and chatting up boys after showing off their so called dance moves that would make an epileptic embarrassed.

In the corner of the bar, well away from the likes of the future CEO's of America in their polo shirts and Nantucket reds, Francis and his "Cousins" were sitting in a booth discussing some recent events that had taken place.

"Have you thought of a name for it yet?" one of the cousins asked.

"I was toying with the idea of FX's Hell."

"FX huh? You were always such a humble bastard, you know that?" They all laughed. Sitting next to Francis were three of his gorgeous female friends, Vanna, Christine and Ashley. Francis resembled an Irish Hugh Hefner; however, he had no attraction to any of them.

"Well, we might as well do a shot to commemorate," Ashley said.

"Absolutely," Francis replied. "To FX's Hell, they'll sure get a bang out of that!"

"You're a fuckin' lousy comedian, you know?" Christine laughed.

As the merriment continued, Francis noticed a beautiful black girl from the corner of his eye and watched as she approached the bar. He excused himself from his delightful conversation with his "Cousins" and walked up to her.

"Hello. There is no reason a beautiful woman like you needs to drink alone. Won't you join us?" Francis said, flashing his winning smile.

"No, no. It's quite alright. Thank you anyways," the girl softly replied.

"What's your name?"

"Michelle...Michelle Patrick."

"What a pretty name. I'm Francis X. O'Donnell. Tell me, where are you from?"

"Woburn."

"Woburn, huh? It's funny, I feel like I might have known you before. Perhaps in a different life right?"

Michelle smiled shyly. The truth was Francis knew that she was from Woburn, knew her name was Michelle Patrick, and knew she lived with her mother and brother. He knew her father was dead, that she was born in Haiti and moved to the U.S. when she was two years old. He knew that her blood type was O positive. In fact, it was safe to say Francis may have known more about Michelle than she knew about herself. This was no act of fate that Francis knew where to meet her. Michelle and he had met for a reason. For Michelle was about to play a very important role in Francis Xavier's plan.

"The Cousins" did not seem at all phased when Francis brought Michelle back to the table. The group carried on and enjoyed their remedies with natural merriment for the Irish are never without friends in a bar.

"Do you know what I've realized in all my years on this earth?"

Matt Gallagher said in a drunken slur. "I've never gone to bed with an ugly woman ever!" The crowd laughed, and to their chuckles he replied, "But I've woken up with plenty."

Michelle felt uneasy with the crass comments being made at the table but continued to stay and engage in conversation with the charming Irish Bostonian she had just met. By the end of the night, she seemed enamored in her new friend; the two exchanged phone numbers.

****

Over the next few weeks, Francis and Michelle stayed in close contact. Francis would send her a text just checking in on her day, and Michelle would always reply back and ask how his was in return. His response was always… "better now." After numerous coy text messages, the two decided to rendezvous.

One night they were walking home from dinner through the streets of Boston. The city in the summer time has a charmingly humid appeal that entices one to lose clothing before arriving to the bedroom. That night was no different.

The two walked hand and hand through the cobblestone streets. As Francis was about to leave Michelle at the train, he stopped and looked her in the eyes and passionately kissed her; the type of kiss she had only seen in the movies and usually involved fireworks or a fairy godmother. Michelle did not get on the train. Instead, she and Francis spent a passionate night together at his condo.

When Michelle awoke the next morning, Francis had a full Irish breakfast waiting for her in the kitchen.

A few days later the two were having a wonderful dinner in the posh Boston suburb of Brookline. There weren't many places in the greater Boston area that weren't infested with the influx of drunken college students. Brookline, while wonderful, was the most affected. It housed Boston University: home of the future prostitutes and tax evaders of America wearing their Birkenstocks and pearl earrings.

At the table next to them were three young college students. Using their parent's credit cards to enjoy drinks and food at the establishment, they didn't give much regard to anyone else around them. When Michelle and Francis sat down, one of the college kids whispered loudly, "Wow look, the maid and chauffer must have the night off." The table began to laugh at their superiority towards their company. Francis got up and walked over to the table. He looked the boy straight in the eye and said, "I hope to God you have good health insurance; one that covers teeth and broken noses, because if one of you so much as makes a peep, you're going to need it."

The students looked at Francis in fear while he glared at them with eyes like pits of fire from hell burning a hole through their souls with an unparallel evil, the likes which none of those assholes had ever seen. Francis sat back down.   Michelle looked frightened. "There was something in your eyes right then," she said. "Something I've never seen before." Francis just sat there, watching the boys scurry out of the restaurant.

"Well, I guess you've just never seen me mad."

"They are probably outside waiting for you."

"One can only hope."

On their walk home, Francis revealed some disturbing news to Michelle. "I'm being called away on business in Europe for a few weeks." Michelle looked disappointed, but held Francis' hand.

"I guess we better make the best of tonight", she said. They returned to Francis' home, however, the next morning she awoke to an empty bed. Lying beside her was a note and a rose. "Think of me when you smell this but know that a field of these could not compare to your beauty."

He was thoughtful. She was in love.

Chapter 9

The overhead speaker turned on. "Ladies and gentleman, the Captain has turned on the fasten seatbelt sign indicating final decent into London Heathrow Airport. We ask that you place your seat backs and tray tables in their full, upright and locked position."

The wheels touched down on the tarmac and Francis exited the plane. He stopped and looked around at the behemoth airport. "Welcome to garbage," he thought the sign should say as he proceeded to the baggage claim and customs.

He hadn't stepped two feet outside of the terminal when he saw the awaiting Mercedes. Once in the passenger seat, he looked at the stern woman next to him: a shrewd and cold feminine creature with equally black features and the same piercing eyes doting under her Chanel sunglasses.

"You look like you had a rough flight, or are you just getting old?" she asked with a smirk.

"Doesn't matter how old I get sister dear, I'll always be younger than you."

The car drove towards City Centre. When they arrived at his sister's house, another woman greeted them at the door.

"Good morning Matthew!" Francis said with a smirk.

"It's Mary, and if you're going to start you might as well turn back around and head home. I'm sure there is some tart flight attendant just dying to catch you on your outbound flight."

Francis laughed and said, "Ah, perhaps but they would never have your natural beauty. Remind me again what breed you are?" Francis then entered the house while Kathleen grabbed her brother's luggage. She looked around at her nosey neighbors and slyly shut the door. The agenda was tight for the day: sandwiches, tea, and murder.

Chapter 10

The latched door shut with a slam as Sergeant Johnson sat fixed on the television. While the images of a vintage Judi Dench flashed across the screen, Johnson could not help but to chuckle and weep all at the same time. Could it have been karma that caused him to be paralyzed and be remanded to the aid of a wheelchair for the remainder of his days? A wheelchair that due to his ailment, was controlled only by his fingers.

Even though he still spent every waking hour with the woman he had been married to for fifty years, he was still alone. Perhaps it was the distance he felt from her, or maybe it was because of the years of repented guilt. Perhaps it was the longing of his conscious to free him from his past before his days were over, or was it simply because he really was alone ever since his wife started volunteering at a library for hours at a time and, on top of that, began a drinking habit. Johnson, however, could not express his sins even if he chose to do so. He could neither speak nor write due to his paralyzing illness. The only comfort he had was his visiting aide that would arrive at his home every day from 11:00 a.m. and stay until to 1:00 p.m.

Francis already knew all of this information. In fact, Francis had been keeping track of Sergeant Johnson for some time now to formulate the exact time to pay him a visit. The next day at 12:55 p.m., Sergeant Johnson watched his aide leave him and he returned to his shows. Suddenly, the door opened again and standing in front of him was Francis, disguised as a delivery man dressed in uniform and carrying a box.

"Sorry to startle you sir. The health aide told me to just come right in. Got a package for you."

Francis approached Johnson who had both arms held to his electronic wheelchair with Velcro straps which enabled him to control the chair with buttons at his finger tips. He also had access to a panic button near his right hand. Before he had a chance to react, Francis released both straps causing Johnson's arms to fall useless to the side of the chair.

"You killed Barney O'Donnell with the other two assholes, you fuckin' wanker. They got theirs, and now sir, you will get yours." His words were chilling, even to a man who could not feel. Francis continued, "I want you to think long and hard about what you did and how you stabbed a knife in his neck." Francis took a razor sharp blade out from the delivery box and held it in front of the man's neck and slowly applied pressure.

Francis reminded Johnson that he had not said a word during Barney O'Donnell's suicide investigation, knowing Barney had been murdered. He told Johnson that maybe if he had two mouths, he could have said something. He continued on and told Johnson he hoped his trip to hell was slow and painful. The last thing he told Johnson before giving him his second mouth was that when his wife came home he would kill her and his two granddaughters. Johnson wet his pants. The knife slid into Johnson's neck like a Christmas ham, and the man began to gasp for his last breath. Francis walked to the door, opened it, and then turned around. Francis then walked back over to what was now Johnson's blood saturated, lifeless body and hit the panic button on his chair. He nodded his head with approval and walked out the door.

On route back to the airport, Francis and Kathleen stopped to have dinner. Francis sat with his sister and, over four pints of Guinness, explained her next mission.

Kathleen smirked, "I haven't been to France in quite some time. It will be as easy as it was putting a third ear in that murdering fuck, Timothy Moore's head."

Francis responded, "Be patient. There is a lot of work ahead of us. There are a lot of people to remind that we didn't forget and a lot of people to make very sorry that they ever cheered for 'Bloody Sunday.' Don't worry though...I have it all under control."

Chapter 11

Springtime in Boston can be a conundrum. One must be prepared for the myriad of seasonal elements. And, while one day can sprout blossoms with a hint of a summer breeze, the next day can begin with a blizzard to kill what had begun to bloom.

Michelle and Francis were strolling down the Esplanade when Francis noticed a girl wearing a Red Sox hat over her face and large sunglasses. Even through the concealed adornment, Francis recognized her as his cousin's daughter, Maura. He approached her and inquired about her plight.

"Why are you hiding?"

The girl took her sunglasses off to reveal a large swollen black eye.

"Wow," Francis said. "You look like you were at the end of a losing fight."

Tears welled up in Maura's eyes. She then sat down on the end of the bench and regained her composure. "Cousin Francis, I was in the club the other night and there was a guy groping my friend on the dance floor and making her very uncomfortable. I tried to get her away from him, but when I did he threw me up against the wall and hit me. I finally got a bouncer to help me and when they were taking the guy out of the club, he was screaming, 'Do you know who I am?!' We were so scared we had to get a bouncer to walk us to our car in case he was waiting for us. I was just trying to do the right thing and ended up getting hurt," she sobbed.

Michelle watched as Francis once again amazed her with his unrequited love for his family.

"Maura, you're my cousin's daughter and we will take care of you. Tell your father to call me."

And with that, he gave the girl a kiss on the forehead and sent her off. As Michelle and Francis walked towards North Station, Michelle turned to him and said, "You took an interest in her."

"Yes, that is my cousin Paddy Doherty's daughter. Speaking of taking interest…how is your brother? Wasn't he trying to get out of some debt a little while ago?"

"Well you know him. Once he gets his paycheck, it's all gone in a week. He just can't seem to keep a stable job."

"Why don't you let me make some phone calls on his behalf and I will get back to you."

Francis gave Michelle one last kiss in front of the train station and saw her off. As he continued home to his two million dollar waterfront condo, Francis began to think about his cousin's daughter. The thoughts angered him and, no sooner than he arrived home, he called Paddy and left a voicemail. "Pdiragh ol' boy, when you get this, come over straight away. Don't call. I'm thinking that I'm about to cause a lot of trouble for the bastard who put his hands on Maura and I need your help. Don't worry…I have a plan."

Later that evening, Francis met with Paddy Doherty, Tim McHugh and Tom Sullivan. He discussed the events that caused Paddy's daughter to be injured. Francis told the trio that he wanted all the information that they could gather on the wise guy and his friends. Paddy told FX that he had a lot of information already, because he planned to take care of the bastard himself. He wasn't going to bother Francis. The guy who had hit Maura was the son of a former politician from Boston who now owned a large auto dealership in the City of Waltham. His son and one of the other morons that were with him that night also work at the dealership.

The third guy that was with them worked for the transit authority in some bullshit political job.

The wise ass son thinks he's a playboy. He has a thirty-seven foot boat that he keeps in a Mystic River marina. On most Sundays, he and his two asshole buddies, along with a few female escorts or whores, can be found around Boston Harbor. He likes to anchor about two thousand yards or so off Castle Island near the end or one of the Logan Airport runways so that he can drink and play games with the ladies.

Francis remarked, "You have already done your homework on this guy. It will definitely make things a little bit easier. My thoughts are that we should have a little picnic on Castle Island some Sunday very soon."

The forecast for the third Sunday in June was for a warm clear day...just the right weather for a picnic. Francis arranged for those from his inner circle in the Boston area and a few "Cousins" from Ireland to attend the Castle Island party.

As the day went on, Francis noted that although most of the folks attending the party had knowledge of his "FX's Hell" demonstration in New Hampshire, some had never actually seen it work.

Early on that Sunday morning, Sully and McHugh had visited the marina where Mr. Wise Guy stored his boat. They brought with them a small bottle of "FX's Hell" which they poured on the rear of the boat just above the fuel tank.

Francis asked his group to direct their attention to the boat with large black stripes that was moored on the harbor about two thousand yards away from them. On the deck, they could see three men and a few girls in bikinis. Francis took what looked like two remote controls for a TV. He told his folks that what they were about to see would brighten up their day and the people on the boat would get a "bang" out of it. He pointed the controls in the direction of the boat and within seconds, there was the sound of the explosion, and all that could be seen was smoke and a large fire ball. The boat was merely splinters.

Every boat in the area rushed to the scene: pleasure boats, coast guard boats, fire and police boats. The only thing they found was debris and body parts.

Francis and the group thought it was a great show. They enjoyed the rest of the day watching all the activity that was taking place in the water.

McHugh asked Francis, "What were you humming while all the excitement was going on?"

"Just a little Patsy Cline song," Francis said, called, "I Fall to Pieces."

"Francis my boy, your heart is always in the right place," laughed McHugh.

The next day the newspapers were full of stories about the tragedy on the harbor. How sad it was that such wonderful people were killed in what the Coast Guard described as, "a terrible accident which most likely was caused by an electrical problem from the fans near the fuel tank."

Paddy Doherty and his daughter Maura were reading about the tragedy. Paddy remarked to his daughter, "Mr. Wise Guy and his friends met a tragic end. God works in mysterious ways."

"So does Francis X," Maura replied.

"What do you mean by that?"

"Oh, nothing."

They both just smiled.

Chapter 12

Francis was excited to meet Joseph Patrick. He felt as though the two of them were going to have a lot in common, if not now, than certainly in the future. They met at one of the most upscale restaurants in Boston. Michelle, Joseph, and Francis X. all sat down for a nice meal.

"So you're the guy who has been seeing my sister, huh? What are you looking for?"

Joseph's attitude was exactly what Francis thought it might be, rough but empty. He was a bit of a smart ass and that worked perfectly for Francis.

"I have been seeing your sister. I care for her very much. In fact, I care for her so much that I want to help you out."

"What if I don't want your help?"

"Joseph!" Michelle said startled. "Behave yourself. We talked about this."

"No, no Michelle it's quite alright," said Francis. "I seemed to have overstepped my boundaries. Why don't we just enjoy this dinner and call it a day, huh? I mean, you sir are clearly more than capable of supporting yourself and carrying your own weight in your mother's house. I'm sure you don't cause her any stress at all, what with not having a job and having her pay for all your bills the same way she did since you were born. You don't need me to help you back on your feet and get you permanently financially stable. You seem just fine. So carry on. You clearly know better than I." Francis' eyes never once waivered away from Joseph's.

"I'm listening Paddy."

"Actually, Paddy is my cousin and I'll let that one slide. You get to use that card once and you just did."

The two sat with a dead stare with each other, and Michelle was afraid their combined tempers might be too volatile for a public setting. She wondered how on earth Francis was ever going to want to see her again, let alone give her brother a job.

Joseph reached down for the menu, all the while looking into Francis' eyes and Francis did the same. Their menus opened but their eyes stayed fixated on one another. Finally, Joseph spoke.

"I imagine you're going to order a Guinness?"

"Only if it's for you," Francis replied. "I will take a shot of tequila, specifically Patron."

Joseph smiled and so did Francis. Michelle let out a sigh of relief. Not much eating was done at the meeting, but a lot of drinking certainly took place. One shot of Patron after another and, as the night went on, Michelle felt as though she had stumbled into the Boy's Club, watching the man she cared for very much and the man that cared for her so very much get along so well. There was laughing and singing, and an equal love for the Red Sox and hatred for the New York Yankees among other things that caused Francis and Joseph to get along so well. Francis slammed the shot glass down and looked in Joseph's eyes.

"I want you to make some money for me."

"How much money are we talking about?"

"That depends. How much money do you want to make? You are in control of your own income. You want to make five thousand dollars a month? Make five thousand. You want to make twenty thousand? Make twenty thousand. Hell, make twenty million dollars!" Francis was slurring his words and making quite the spectacle of himself.

Michelle intervened. "Francis, I don't think you should be

discussing business right now. You've had a little too much to drink."

Francis picked Michelle up as though they were ready to waltz. "Joseph, I see your sister got both the looks and the brains in your family. Tell you what. Why don't you come into my office next week and we'll sort this out and make you some money."

Joseph laughed and stood up, shook Francis' hand and nearly fell over drunk. You've got yourself a meeting sir. Why don't you make sure you got the tea and crumpets ready when I come over."

"Tea and crumpets!? Do you hear him Michelle?! Ingrate! I'd rather be called 'Paddy' than insult me in the manner he just did."

The three left the restaurant and stumbled down the street with each one of the men on Michelle's arms. As they made it to a cab stand, Michelle and Joseph got into a cab bound for home. Francis leaned up against the cab stand pole and waved as they drove away. Once the cab was out of sight, he then stood upright and proceeded to walk straight home without the slightest sway or limp. It was an almost cocky stride that led him to the front door of his condo.

Chapter 13

A few weeks had passed and Francis began to wonder if Joseph Patrick was going to follow through or not. He had no intention of pursuing the issue with Michelle at this point; the majority of her role in Francis' life was done. While that was the case, Francis kept her around for special circumstances and the like. About three weeks after the meeting with Joseph, his phone rang; it was the man himself.

"Mr. O'Donnell, this is Joseph Patrick, Michelle's brother. I was wondering about that meeting."

Francis put his cup of tea down and replied, "Joseph, have you ever heard the phrase, 'The early bird catches the worm?' Well, there is another phrase by the same author," he went on to say, "The lazy bastard who can't get off his fat ass to make phone calls gets no money." Francis then slammed down the phone.

Francis always thought his jokes were funny. He proceeded to count backwards, "ten, nine, eight." The phone rang again.

"Impatient little bastard, aren't you?" Francis said as he picked up the phone.

"Mr. O'Donnell, please don't hang up," the frustrated voice on the other end pleaded. "I promise, I will do whatever you want. No questions asked. Just please, please let me work for you."

Francis took the opportunity to let the smart ass know just who the boss was. "Be here in ten minutes or you will never hear from me again."

"Ten minutes! But I live about twenty-five away!"

"That wasn't a question," Francis coldly responded and hung up the phone.

The clock on the wall read nine minutes since Francis cut off communication with Joseph. It was intriguing and stressful to wonder if Joseph was going to make it on time. Francis knew his plan was useless without Joseph, but the stubborn Irish in him was not going to let some unemployed fucker dictate where and when his meetings were going to take place.

Ten minutes had passed and Francis started to grow angry. Eleven minutes had gone by and then there was a knock at the door. Francis opened it to reveal a heaving and wheezing Joseph Patrick.

"You're late. Come in."

The two sat down as Joseph looked around the condo in astonishment.

"Wow! Nice place you got here."

"It's called hard work. You could have one too if you got yourself some work."

"Alright, look man, I know you're upset, but I wasn't sure if you were feeding me a bunch of bullshit. I mean you just show up out of nowhere, offer me a job and that's it?"

"Well, you don't even know what the job is yet."

"Yes I do, my sister was telling me…something about a lobster boat."

"Do you really think I would take my time to find you and talk to you if I wanted a lobster? Look outside. I live right next to Legal Seafood. I'm good."

Joseph looked confused as Francis began to explain. "I know a lot about you Joseph Patrick. I know you were in the United States

Marine Corps for seven weeks before being discharged. I know that you've had minor scrapes with the law and that you are down on your luck. I think I can help you if you want to help me, but I need your complete trust and confidentiality on the matter."

Joseph looked stunned. Who was this man, and how did he know so much about him?

Francis continued. "The lobster boat was just a cover story, but the money was no lie. Joseph Patrick, I can guarantee you sixty thousand dollars at the end of this trip if you agree. It may only take three months. It may take four. However, all of your expenses will be paid."

The amount of money rattled Joseph's brain. That was more money than he had earned in his life! He was hesitant to even question it.

"So what do you want me to do? Kill someone?"

"Now why would I want you to do that? Take this." Francis handed him a United States passport with Joseph's picture, but with a different name. He also handed him a piece of paper with an address that was just outside Dublin and a picture of a young woman. Francis continued. "I know this does not make sense now, but I assure you it will. Are you interested?"

"Yes…absolutely!" Joseph replied without any hesitation.

Francis cautioned. "Joseph, this isn't a game. What you are entering into is a very serious matter, and I have no patience or room for failure. I need one hundred percent of your commitment the entire time. I will not tolerate anything less!"

"You have nothing to worry about. I'll do anything."

Francis felt confident in his decision. "I will meet you in two weeks and let you know the final details. Until then, begin to say your goodbyes to your family and friends and let them know how excited you are to start your new job on the lobster boat on Prince Edward Island. Remember Joseph, this is extremely confidential. If you fail me, your services will end abruptly. You catch my drift?"

"Yes sir, I understand," Joseph said as he waved goodbye to his newest employer.

Everyone that Francis worked with was important to him, but no one at this point was more vital to his plan than the man who just walked out of his front door. Francis had a lot of work ahead of him, but wasn't worried. As always…Francis X had a plan.

Chapter 14

The murky air in Ireland had a different feel to it today. A place of exceptionally good spirit and familiarity was now a place of deceit and demise.

Joseph Patrick did not have the same first experience in Ireland that most people have, for when his plane touched down in Belfast International Airport, his life changed, and not for the better.

Joseph was given specific instructions from Francis' associates and was greeted at the airport by Colin O'Neil and Desmond Kelly, two of Francis' most trusted colleagues in the north. As they drove to a small hotel just outside Belfast, Joseph began to feel more like a prisoner and less like a worker. The two men sat in silence in the front seat of the van. Any words that were said were muddled by an accent that Joseph was not accustomed to and, being from Boston, that was no small fete.

The next few weeks were a blur. Each day was another school lesson taught by the fiercest teachers. Culture, language, geography, etiquette, and of course bar manners, were forced into Joseph's head at lightning speed. All too soon, he was ready for his mission and Francis was happy to be informed of his great progress.

Francis was ready for the next step in his plan and hung up

the phone. He picked it up again and rang back a rental agent. Soon, Joseph was ready to move into his own home in Bray, a small waterside suburb of Dublin. He would not be moving into this place as Joseph Patrick; instead, he would be taking the final steps toward leaving the life he had always known. From now own, he would be working and living in Dublin, Ireland as Joseph Michael Parker and it would be at the house in Bray where the wheels of Francis' plan began to turn.

Chapter 15

Kayleigh Clark was a twenty-one year old woman going to University in Dublin. Originally from Waterford, Kayleigh was a beautiful young girl with auburn hair and large green eyes. Although many people would say she was stunningly beautiful, Kayleigh was never one to attract attention. She lived a quiet life, balancing her studies with a job at a department store just off O'Connell Street. Each morning, she would ride her bike from her apartment in Merrimont to Landsdown train station where she would take a train to Dublin City Centre to attend school and work her part-time job.

That particular day wasn't any different than other days for Kayleigh. She had just returned from the library and was about to get on her bike to depart for home, when suddenly, a man in a woven cape leaped from the bushes and grabbed her pocket book. She screamed, but was too scared to try and chase the thief. Just then, a man came out from the other side of the station and saw Kayleigh and the perpetrator and he began to chase the thief. The man from the station was much faster than the thief and stopped the perpetrator dead in his tracks. Once the man caught up with the crook and retrieved the purse, the man ran away towards the setting sun of Dublin.

Out of breath, the man from the station did not bother to chase the thief any further, since he had achieved his goal of retrieving the stolen purse. Kayleigh quickly caught up to the man to thank him.

"Oh my! Thank you so much sir. You don't understand, all of my semester exams and money are in this bag and I would've been lost without it!" Kayleigh exclaimed in a brogue stereotypical of a wee Irish lass.

The man replied, "My pleasure ma'am. I heard your scream and thought you were in need of some assistance."

His accent was standard American with an effected twang of an accent she had never heard before. They walked towards the Jury's Towers, talking, laughing and making general small talk. She introduced herself as Kayleigh Clarke, an aspiring nurse. He replied with his own introduction: Joseph Parker, a United States Marine stationed at the American Embassy in Dublin just down the road from the very train station they had first encountered each other. Kayleigh was grateful to Mr. Parker for his help and bid him farewell. As she began to leave on her bicycle, he stopped her.

"Can I see you again Ms. Clarke? If only for tea, I would be honored to have your company." His words so soft and polite, and his accent was adorable to her.

"That would be lovely. How about tomorrow? Same time, but not the same place," Kayleigh said as she got on her bike and headed home.

Joseph chuckled as he reached into his pocket, took out his mobile phone and texted "all set" to the only number he had stored. He then returned to the train station and caught the next train back to Bray.

The next day, the two met for tea at a small shop near the American Embassy. Kayleigh was intrigued with Joseph's ornately decorated Marine Corps uniform while he spent time explaining all the different types of badges, pins and patches from the different positions he had been in. (It should be noted that U.S. Embassy Marine Security Guard members rarely wore their uniform outside of the Embassy).

"You've really guarded the President of the United States?!" she said, awestruck.

"Yup, it was pretty interesting, but not as interesting as my time in the Middle East though. Seeing my friends, my brothers in arms leave with me from the United States and not have all of them return home was really tough." Joseph started to choke up and saw tears form in Kayleigh's eyes.

"I'm so sorry Joseph. I promise there is something better for you in the future."

"I hope so," he said as he grabbed her hand while looking her in the eyes. She began to blush.

Chapter 16

In Londonderry lived a young boy from Waterford who worked at a posh hotel called the Evergreen right on the Strand Road. The money he earned was used to pay for his tuition at the University. He had been fortunate to be able to attend a nice Catholic school. He had just finished checking in two guests when the lobby door of the hotel swung open violently and two intimidating British Military police officers marched forcefully into the lobby.

One of the men asked, "Where is Liam O'Reilly?"

"I am Liam O'Reilly," the boy said. His words were shaking.

"Sir, you are going to have to come with us. We have to ask you some questions about a recent crime committed at St. Columb's University. It's a grave situation, and I'm afraid you are the main suspect."

The boy's managers looked at Liam shamefully. He always seemed like such a hard worker, and they could not fathom him committing any crimes at all. Liam grabbed his coat and walked out the door with the military police officers... and never to return.

At the end of the night, one of the cooks was emptying out some of the garbage in the alley next to the hotel. He heard a moan. There, lying in the pool of his own blood was what was left of Liam

O'Reilly; beaten to hell and on the brink of death. His father, the prominent Liam O'Reilly Sr. of Waterford rushed up to Derry to be by his son's side in the hospital. His father could not understand why the British MP's would target his boy.

The next day his father went to the barracks on the outskirts of town and demanded to know what had happened. The only information he knew was that two British soldiers had brutally beaten his son and left him for dead outside of a Derry hotel. The Corporal in charge of the barracks assured Mr. O'Reilly that there were no MP's scheduled in that area. O'Reilly was sure that someone was lying, but he was told that he was indeed "shrewdly mistaken." Outraged and confused, O'Reilly stayed in the North for four days before returning to Waterford feeling helpless and defeated.

There is one thing to note about the Irish, and that is that they do not give up very easily and humility is not one of their strong suits.

The father returned to work at the Waterford Crystal factory, a job that had been in his family for three generations. Master craftsmen at Waterford were regarded as highly as leather shoe makers in Italy. They were seen more as artists than they were as tradesman.

It took the hospital in Derry three weeks to get the boy stable enough to be transferred to a hospital in Cork. Only nineteen years old and on the brink of death, Mr. O'Reilly was ready to kill whoever it was that did this to his boy, no matter what it cost.

Peter Clark of Waterford joined O'Reilly every day after their shift at the famed Waterford drinking establishment O'Donnell Kells II. W.D. O'Donnell-Proprietor. This quaint little pub on the quay was frequented by fisherman, tourists, and the locals. It was known for its hearty food, hooley nights, and relaxed atmosphere.

The manager of the pub, a stout man by the name of John Fahy, happened to be one a first cousins to Francis Xavier, and a member of his "inner circle." Always one with a story or a bit of life wisdom, he was respected and frequently visited by the workers at Waterford Crystal.

That day O'Reilly and Clark came in solemn. Fahy asked the status of O'Reilly's son.

"How's he doin' there Liam? Any progress?"

"Aye, the doctors got the final tests back," Liam said as the Guinness pressed against his lips. "He's in a coma for God knows how long. If he makes it out, he's going to be a vegetable." Before John could reply, Liam was ordering another larger. He finished off his first beer and slammed his glass against the bar and shouted, "Fuckin' British Bastards!"

"It isn't right!" John said. "Something needs to be done Liam. If it were my son, I'd have something done about it."

****

Back in Bray, Desmond and Collin were planning their next move for Kayleigh Clarke. Up until now, they were content with Joseph seeing her on a cordial basis, but now it was time to push their plan into action. They instructed Joseph to have Kayleigh meet him outside of the U.S. Embassy at 42 Eglin Road, right down the street from where she lived, and so he did.

The sun was setting early on the Irish capital and, sure enough, at 6 p.m. there was Joseph, dressed to impress in his shiny uniform. He grabbed his lady by the arm and escorted her to dinner. That dinner led to another dinner, then a lunch, then tea, then the theatre, and then as with most young romances, it led to the bedroom.

At this point, he was comfortable enough to report back to Desmond and Colin and she was comfortable enough to call him her boyfriend. The same situation, but two distinctly different mindsets. Soon, the two started to go away together for long weekends. Taking in the Cliffs of Moher on the Clare coast and then up to Giant's Causeway in the north. They felt the Irish countryside was their giant playground; she started to fall in love. A few months later, however, her love soon turned to fear. She came to meet Joseph one day with a frightened look on her face and a shaking in her hand.

"What's the matter baby? Did someone die?"

She shook her head no in response.

"Well then, what? Don't worry. Whatever it is you can tell me." His words were comforting. She wiped the tears from her eyes and looked at him. "I'm pregnant."

He smiled almost joyously. "Don't worry about that babe, I would happily marry you." His words comforted her no longer.

"There's a problem. I don't know how my parents will react. I have never actually told them I was seeing you."

"What do you think they'll more of a problem with, me being black or me being American?"

"I don't really know which one they will think is worse to be honest."

"Does it count for nothing that I've served in my country and am now serving in yours? That I fought so that nations like Ireland could be free and beautiful women like you could have babies without social segregation or alienation? Have I done all of that for nothing?" He put his head between his hands as if to sob.

She rushed to his side to comfort him. "You're right. It's a modern day and there is nothing that should keep us apart. If God meant for us to have a child together then so be it. My parents will have to accept it." She kissed him on the head and they went to sleep.

The next day, Joseph told Kayleigh that he had received an urgent letter from his Commander saying that he was needed in Garmisch, Germany for special training. He told her that he would be back soon and he gave her a USMC sweatshirt and a picture of him. It was a headshot of him at Marine Corps boot camp with an American flag waving in the background. He told her to keep them and they would bring comfort to her. He then kissed her goodbye and told her he'd see her soon. She kissed him back and shut the door to the cab as it drove away. It would be the last time she would ever see him.

Days passed, then a week, then ten days. Kayleigh started to panic. What if something happened to him at training? What if he decided not to come back to Ireland? What if he did not love her anymore? The thoughts pained Kayleigh's head and she became depressed, locking herself in her room for days at a time with only his picture and sweatshirt and their unborn child.

Frantic, she called her sister and told her the entire story. Her sister knew there was only one option: she had to get an abortion.

"I couldn't possibly!" Kayleigh said to her sister on the phone. "What would Mom and Dad think?"

"That its better you get an abortion than give birth to a half black baby! Jesus Kayleigh…think about it! You haven't heard from him in weeks. He doesn't want this baby and what kind of a life will it have if the kid's grandparents won't even accept it as a bastard. Besides, I'll pay for the whole thing. I know you aren't in the best place financially, but Jesus, we have to do something."

Kayleigh sadly agreed and within a few days she was in Dublin at the women's clinic terminating the pregnancy.

Kayleigh returned home to mourn in silence at her apartment. A feeling of remorse set over her. She phoned her sister to let her know that she as okay and that she would ring her soon. Her sister had not heard from her in several days so in a panic, she made her way to Dublin to check on Kayleigh. She phoned some of Kayleigh's friends en route; however, she found that none had been in touch with Kayleigh for days. Then, the unthinkable happened, when she went to Kayleigh's apartment. She opened the door with the spare set of keys that Kayleigh had given to her and found Kayleigh's body nearly rotted on her bed. Kayleigh's lower part of her body was covered in blood and her sister quickly dialed the police.

Upon investigation, Kayleigh's death was determined to be a hemorrhage caused from the botched abortion.

Her mother was hysterical, but the person struck with most grief was her sister for suggesting that she even go through with it. The coroner took most of her belongings out of the room when the body was removed, but her sister could not help but notice a picture lying on the side of the bed. It was a picture of a United States Marine. She took it with her before seeing the remains of her sister being wheeled out.

Funeral arrangements were made in Waterford for the following Thursday, and half the city showed up to pay their respects to the Clarke family.

Kayleigh's father, Peter, was a large man, over six feet tall, and no one could recall ever seeing such a strong man whimper so much at the loss of his baby girl. Peter Clarke was truly inconsolable.

Several weeks later, Peter went to the American Embassy in Dublin in an attempt to find the man who he believed was responsible for his daughter's medical decision and, in Peter's mind, her life. He knew the man's name was Joseph Parker, however, when he attempted to get information, he was quickly dismissed by the Marine Guard commander who claimed that no one by that name had ever worked for the United States Embassy and certainly no one resembled the picture at hand. He then talked with the attaché's office who said there was nothing they could do. Outraged, Peter stormed away from the round building and slamming his fist onto the Dublin road screamed. "If I had a bomb, I would blow this ugly fucking place up!" He was sure they were covering up for their own. These Americans, he thought, "nothing can be their fault."

He stayed in Dublin for days searching coffee shops, pubs, and asking anyone if they had seen the man in the picture, Joseph Parker. He left Dublin sad and defeated. He longed for answers, but could only relish in grief and sorrow. He wasn't sure what he could do, but he knew that something had to be done.

A few days had passed since Peter Clarke had returned home and found himself in the one place he knew that he could seek solace: O'Donnell's Kells II. His counter mate, Liam O'Reilly, was another Waterford man who also knew the pain of having a child taken from him. O'Reilly sat facing Peter and the two commiserated about their family anguish. The mediator to this conversation was none other than John Fahy, who heard the complaints of his patrons and friends and knew exactly what he could provide to assuage their frustration.

"Gentleman, I realize you are both rightfully upset and your families have been wronged. Liam, the British had no right taking your boy's wits from him. He was a good lad and it hurts me to see you upset. Peter, Kayleigh was the light of your life and if those no good fuckin' Yanks want to protect that bastard who did this to her…then they are just as guilty as he is. Don't worry gents, I know some good people in the right places who will be able to take care of those who have wronged you. They got no right doing what they did and believe me, and I swear on me life…they will pay."

With that, he poured three shots of Paddy's Irish whiskey and toasted Liam and Kayleigh and the great things they could have done.

Chapter 17

The sun began to set over the Irish coastline in Bray. For several weeks now, Joseph Patrick had been laying low after leaving Dublin for good. While he was unaware of what had become of Kayleigh Clarke, he knew what he did was wrong and was only hoping to finish his job and receive his money. At the instruction of Francis, Joseph phoned his sister to tell her that he had been on leave from his boating excursion and that he was set to return to sea soon; however, he would be back in two weeks. His family was very relieved to hear from him, but even more happy that he was gainfully employed and keeping out of trouble. Michelle could not help but thank Francis for all of his help, with helping her brother sort out his life; Francis was happy to oblige. Joseph hung up the phone with his sister and felt relieved and anxious at the same time.

That night, Colin and Damon took Joseph in a car and moved him quickly from Bray, hundreds of miles north to the mountains of Donegal, where they stayed for four long weeks. Joseph was convinced that they were there for his own safety and to make sure that when Francis sent over the money they would be close to an airport to receive it and then he could go home. Joseph was quite anxious to spend his earnings.

Several days later, Damon received a phone call and was occupied for a long period of time. When he returned to the living room of the farm house, he gave Joseph a big hug.

"Good news there Joey, just got the phone call that the coast is clear and tomorrow you're on your way home!"

Joseph looked excited and said, "Fantastic! Wait...we have been together for four months and this is the first time you've called me Joey. Does this mean we're friends?"

Damon responded heartily. "Mate, we'll be friends for the rest of our lives."

Colin chimed in, "I hope that it's fifty more years there ya' bastards."

The three men laughed and Joseph returned to his bedroom and began packing. The next day he had all of his belongings in the back of the car and was ready to go.

Colin yelled, "Hey Joseph, can you just run back to house and double check that the door is locked?"

Joseph ran back to the front door and quickly latched the lock. He returned to the car where he was met with two quick bullets to his chest. His dead body fell swiftly to the ground. The two men removed his shirt and took pictures of his face and then of his chest and face. They then wrapped him up in tarp and stuck him in the back of the car. When darkness fell, they took the body down to a construction site where the town was about ready to pour a concrete slab for a new shopping center the next day. As Damon hurried to dig the cold grave, he looked over to see Colin making the sign of the cross over the top of the body.

"What the fuck are you doing?" Damon asked angrily.

"Just want to make sure the poor bastard rests in peace," Colin replied sincerely.

"You shoot a man twice, in the chest, wrap him up in tarp and then bless him? Brilliant! Fucking brilliant! Next thing you know you'll want to make him a tombstone."

The two men laughed and carried on their work.

The next day they were leaving town and stopped by the site to make sure the rest of the project was carried out. With a stick they carved in the wet cement, "RIP JP." Joseph Patrick was going to have the grandest tombstone in all of Ireland.

Chapter 18

The nightlife in Derry was a bustle as usual. The city brings out a myriad of bar patrons on any given weeknight and tonight was no different, from the glamazons heading to Earth and Sugar to the grandfathers retiring for one more drink at DaVinci's before calling it a night with their women. Of course, there is always lowlife in every city and Derry had seen its share. On that night, two men by the names of Peter Callahan and Adam Brophy were continuing to be the scum of the earth that their parents had raised them to be. Like some of the worst types of people, arrogant and anti-Catholic, they roamed the streets with that feeling of invincibility that all twenty-somethings exude, but few can prove.

They rolled into the Metro Bar ready for a night of rowdy trouble. Immediately, the head bouncer Tania told the boys that if they started any trouble they'd be out. Attempting to keep a low profile, they headed to a corner table and ordered drinks. They quickly downed the first round and were ready for the second. As Peter went to the bar, he noticed two very attractive girls sitting at a table on the other side of the club. Peter nudged Brian, and the two cockily strolled over to the table to introduce themselves.

"Right, haven't seen you two around here before," Brian suavely opened with.

"That's because we aren't from around here," one of the girls replied glancing down at her suitcase.

"Where ya from?"

"Dublin."

"That's a shit city."

"That coming from a Derry lad? You've got some nerve."

The four began to laugh and joke and ordered some more drinks.

"I'm Brian and this sexy bastard to my right is Peter."

"Nice to meet ye. I'm Clare and this here is Alana."

The truth was their names were not Clare and Alana, but they were from Dublin. They worked for a travel agency there, run by none other than Francis Xavier and they were also two close members of his inner circle.

"You know, Peter has an amazing flat overlooking the river. You two should come check it out!"

The girls looked at each other and giggled. The two lads looked approvingly at the situation and the evening was about to get far better than they had anticipated.

After leaving the bar, they went to Peter's flat where the girls expressed that they were hungry.

"Right, we'll go pick up a pizza, eh ladies?"

They agreed that Alana and Brian would go get pizza while Clare and Peter stayed back at the flat.

When they returned with the pizza, Brian asked Clare where Peter was. Coyly she replied, "we had a great time and he passed out."

"That bastard! Falling asleep on such a good night. Oh well, more for me!"

With that, the three poured some wine and started to chat. About twenty minutes into the conversation, Brian's eyes slammed shut and his body fell to the floor. The girls casually went over to their suitcase, took out uniforms resembling British military uniforms and ID cards. They left the pizza and the wine, walked outside and headed to the station to catch a train back to Dublin.

Days later, after tests came back on the two men's bodies, the coroner was speaking to the chief of police and noted, "they had enough poison in them to take down an elephant." The police had discovered the two fake military IDs and immediately matched them up with the two soldiers who had brutally beat up Liam O'Reilly Jr. The coroner ruled the deaths a "double suicide" and indicated that the two men must have felt so badly about the harm that they had caused Liam, they needed to take their own lives.

****

Back in Waterford, the last patron of O'Donnell's Kells II had just walked out the door. The only people left in the building were the barkeep John Fahy, Mr. O'Reilly and Mr. Clarke. The three men were making small talk when Fahy took out several pictures from a drawer behind the bar and a Derry newspaper with the obituary page open.

"See this here Liam, these are the two lousy fucks that beat your boy. They got what they deserved. And here is Liam's student ID card."

Liam Sr. nodded in awe and approval. He knew that he wanted nothing more than vengeance, but never thought it would be served. Right before his eyes were the two men. The faces, the bodies, and the souls of the two inconsiderate bastards who decided they were going to take from Liam Jr. everything he had going for him. In his mind, Liam Sr. knew that this was the least he would have done to them if he were able to get his hands on them.

"Don't think I forgot about you Peter." And with that he showed Peter Clarke the picture of the black soldier lying dead of gunshot wounds. The soldier that had corrupted his beautiful baby girl, who caused pain and anguish for his entire family and who hid behind his country's flag when he was as much a coward as those bastards he fought against.

"That no good son of a bitch! You are a good man John. How did you get this done?!"

"I told you I know people boys," the bartender replied with a matter of fact tone to his voice.

Liam chimed in, "Well John, not sure what we can do to repay you, but you just say the word and it's done." Peter nodded his head in agreement.

"Well, it's interesting that you should say that boys because I actually need your help. I have a plan…" With those words, John Fahy began to divulge the ultimate activation of hatred and fear using the two wounded fathers as pawns.

****

In Dalkey, Francis Xavier was having a meeting with his inner circle, "The Cousins," as he so affectionately called them. Clare and Alana were there and were happy to explain how their plan came to fruition. Francis expressed his content with their work and noted that there would be something extra in their paychecks to look forward to. The work was never over for Francis Xavier. In fact, in his mind, it was just the beginning.

He explained to his followers as he downed his Martini.

"There is much work to be done friends. The night of 'Bloody Sunday' there were four English officers toasting to the death and disaster that was caused on that day. They too must pay and suffer for our friends and relatives, and here is what we must do. First, here are their names: William Taylor, Gary Jenkins, Albert Palmer and George Barker. Mr. Taylor remained in the British Army and retired as a Brigadier General. The others left the army for jobs in the private sector. My plan is to visit each of these bastards or members of their families all on the same day. One lives in London, one in Brighton Beach, south of London and another in Durham in the North of England near the Scottish border. The fourth lives in Lyon, France near Geneva, Switzerland. As you can see, they are spread out all over. My sister Kathleen wants to go to Lyon, with another girl."

Francis then gave each their assignments for the mission: two to London, two to Durham, two to Brighton Beach.

After the meeting, a few of the group were sitting around talking when one of the guys asked Francis what was the significance of the dumb looking statue on his fire place. Francis explained that it was three monkeys - one with its hands over its mouth, one with its hands over its eyes, and the other with his hands over its ears. Below the figurines were the names: Livingston, Moore, and Johnson. It was in memory of two prison guards and a British Army Sgt. One could not speak, one could not hear, and the other could not see. It was really an inside joke.

Chapter 19

Retired Brigadier Taylor had a daughter who, at the age of eighteen, converted to Catholicism and became a nun. She was the vice principal at a girl's school in Lyon, France. On the evening of the 30th of January, the anniversary of "Bloody Sunday," Brigadier Taylor received a phone call at his home from his daughter. She asked her father to please speak with the woman that she was handing the phone to. The woman took his daughter's phone and asked Mr. Taylor if he knew why this was such a special day? Taylor answered, "no" and was told by the woman that he had a very short memory. The woman then reminded him of the massacre in Derry. Taylor then told the woman on the other end of the phone to get to the point of the phone call. She told him that a lot of innocent people died that day due to his and other British soldier's hatred of the Irish. She also told him that after all these years the tears are still flowing from the relatives of those who were killed on that "Bloody Sunday." Her next words were haunting to the old General.

"I am in a vineyard here in Lyon and I am going to shoot your daughter while you listen to her pleading for her life and then you will know how all the family members suffered when you killed their loved ones."

The next thing Taylor heard was his daughter saying a prayer and the sound of a gun being fired. The woman came back on the phone and told Taylor, "She was a good looking girl and I hope you have an open casket. Have a nice day."

Taylor jumped out of his chair in complete shock. When his wife asked him what was going on, he could not get a word out of his mouth. He then slipped on a scatter rug, fell and his head hit the corner of a table. His wife called emergency services, which responded and took Taylor to the hospital where he was treated for a laceration to his left eye. The hospital staff had a hard time restraining him as he kept ranting and screaming about his daughter being shot. They kept him sedated and admitted him to the hospital for the night.

Back in Lyon, at the vineyard, Taylor's daughter, bound hand and foot, was amazed that she was not hurt by the bullet. One of her captors said, "Your father thinks you're dead and that's just what we wanted him to think so he could go through the trauma that the families in Derry went through on 'Bloody Sunday.' We are going to leave you here for the remainder of the night. The vineyard workers will be here at sunrise and you will be all right until then. Tell your father we said hello."

Taylor and his daughter were reunited the next evening when he was released from the hospital with assurance that his laceration would heal just fine. They were concerned about his mental state and suggested further examination.

Upon returning to his home, the family found a flower box addressed to the General. When it was opened, it was found to contain dead red roses with a note that read: "Dear General Taylor. There are fourteen dead roses in this box; one for every poor soul murdered by you and your soldiers. May you never forget. Get Well Soon…(We hope not)!"

Taylor just sat there with a blank stare. He has been almost incoherent since that day. At his age wounds heal slowly…especially mental wounds.

****

Gary Jenkins another veteran of the massacres in Derry on

"Bloody Sunday" gave up his military career to play professional golf. Jenkins did very well as a golfer and won numerous tournaments. He was recognized around the world as a premier golfer. Jenkins had a home in an exclusive section of Brighton Beach just south of London. He had a wife, two children, and five grandchildren. Although he was long retired from the professional golf circuit, Gary managed to play the game at least two to three times a week. Most people who had dealings with Jenkins thought he was one of the most arrogant people that they had ever met. He did have an attitude and was not well liked in the world of golf.

Although he thought of the Irish people as an inferior race, he did admire their golf courses and played in Ireland quite often. He played a few courses in the north of Ireland in Antrim and Tyrone, but would spend five or six days a month playing on Ireland's west coast.

Jenkins was not much of a family man and said on more than one occasion that the only reason he is alive was to play golf. He further stated that if playing golf came to an end, he would hope to die. When asked about his family, Jenkins said, "They are not the brightest bunch in the world, but they may survive without me, although it would be a struggle."

Ireland's weather changes very fast and very often. It was a very mild January, so Jenkins and two other Brits decided to take advantage of the mild temps and make a trip to Galway for two days of golf. They played on the 29th of January and planned to play again the next day.

After dinner in Galway City, Jenkins' two friends decided to explore some of the noisy bars of Galway. Jenkins went back to his hotel room to relax.

After only minutes in his room, Jenkins heard a knock at his door; he thought it was his friends returning. As he opened the door, Jenkins was suddenly overpowered by two men in some type of uniform. They immobilized him and one man put a needle into Jenkins neck containing a very fast acting drug that put him out instantly. The two men dressed as medics, brought in a wheelchair and secured Jenkins to the chair with restraints. They then wheeled him out of the room and brought him to a service elevator which descended to the ground floor at the rear of the hotel where they were met by a third man who helped place Jenkins in the rear of a van. They had traveled three miles east of Galway City before Jenkins started to move. One of the men in the van said, "Thank God, I thought he was dead!" One of the others said, "Too bad he isn't, it would save us a lot of work."

When Jenkins regained consciousness, he had no idea where he was or what had happened. He then realized that he was strapped in a chair and was sitting inside what appeared to be an old shack. One of his captors asked him if he knew what today's date was.

Jenkins responded, "No…just let me out of here!"

The man said, "Does the 30th of January have any significance to you?" Jenkins yelled, "Hell no! Now let me loose!"

The man then asked Jenkins if "Bloody Sunday" meant anything to him?

Jenkins replied, "Yes…we kicked the Irish criminal's asses!"

With that, the man hit Jenkins so hard that he flipped over with the chair. One man said, "You lousy, limey bastard. I should kill you right now, but that would be the easy way out."

At 8:00 a.m. on January 30th on O'Connell Street in Dublin, the "Garda" discovered a man with bloody bandages on his arm and shoulder lying on a bench. The man was rushed to the city hospital where it was discovered that he had been shot in the right shoulder, right elbow and right wrist. The man was identified as the famous golfer Gary Jenkins. It was apparent from his injuries that he would never play golf again.

Gary Jenkins died on the 17th of March that year.

Francis X. said that it is only fitting that he died on such a great day.

****

Albert Palmer was another officer at Bogside in Derry on January 30,1972. Albert left the Army and went into the construction business with his father. Over the years, Albert amassed a fortune and now lived outside of Durham, a city situated about 250 miles north of

London and 125 miles south of Edinburgh, Scotland. He was now Lord Palmer.

To say Palmer was a pervert would be an understatement. His reputation was well known for miles around Durham. The working girls or whores kept a very safe distance from Palmer. Although he paid well, his sexual desires were bizarre. He lived outside the City of Durham and his estate sat on over a thousand acres of land. From the main road to his home was at least a five minute drive. He had never married and maintained a staff of eight full-time employees. Every Saturday, his entire staff was let off until Monday morning; not because he was a generous employer, but because he wanted the house empty so he could frolic with one or two ladies of the evening. He did require his chauffer to stay on duty for the weekends so that he could go to various areas and hire girls for his boss.

On the 29th of January, Palmer's chauffer/ pimp drove to a city in southern Scotland in an attempt to find girls who did not know of Palmer's reputation. He found just what his boss had requested in a gentleman's club: a young, well built blonde under thirty. He invited her to party with his boss, and he told her she would be paid very well and she would have a great time. To the chauffer, she seemed a little tipsy.

Upon arriving at the Palmer estate, the chauffer unlocked the front door and told the girl to go straight through to the "party" room. As the door closed, the chauffer was suddenly overpowered by two men with a rag that had been saturated with chloroform. The rag was put over his mouth, and he was immediately rendered unconscious. He was bound and placed in the trunk of the car. The two men then used his key to enter the house, where they immediately moved to the "party" room in the rear of the house.

Lord Palmer was just beginning to serve his female guest a drink and was standing at the bar wearing a long white bathrobe. Palmer gasped and started shaking at the sight of the two masked intruders. The girl was told to go out the front door, where a car and driver were waiting.

She muttered, "Thank God, this guy is creepy."

While being driven to Newcastle Airport for a flight to London, then on to Dublin, the girl took off her blond wig and told the driver, "blondes really don't have more fun."

Inside Lord Palmer's house, the two masked intruders told Palmer that this was a robbery and he should do as he was told. They took him to another room that appeared to be a library and told him to remove his robe. He resisted and was slapped in the face with an open hand. He finally complied and inside the pocket of his robe they found a pair of handcuffs with a key.

One of the men remarked, "These will come in handy."

Palmer was extremely overweight and one of the thieves then remarked, "He looks like the Pillsbury Doughboy, only he could use a very large bra."

They both laughed and then got down to business.

Palmer was ordered to move a drape on his wall, which when removed revealed a large safe. He was then told, "We know about the security you have for this safe. One, there is an electric switch that must be pushed before touching the dial. Two, if you dial the wrong number once, it's okay, but if you dial the wrong number the second time, an alarm will be sent to a security company and the police will be called. Three, if you fuck up opening the safe then you will die and not fast. Do you understand?"

Palmer nodded and then proceeded to open the safe without incident.

The safe appeared to have more money than two men could carry, and contained currency from every country in the world. One of the men told Palmer that the tax man would throw a party if he had access to this stash.

They then ordered Palmer back over to his bar and told him to pick up and drink the cocktail he had made for the girl. Palmer started to refuse until one of the men took a knife and moved it in the direction of Palmer's genitalia. Palmer quickly downed the drink. Within minutes, he was doped out of his mind and they put the handcuffs on him and waited for the sunrise.

As daylight filtered through the room, Palmer started to stir. One of the men said, "That was a great drink you mixed the girl, but I think it was a little strong for a tiny thing like her. Look what it did to a perverted bastard your size."

They reminded Palmer of the date, the 30th of January and asked him if he ever thought of "Bloody Sunday?"

Palmer replied, "That was ancient history."

One of the men said, "It may be ancient history to you, but it's not to the relatives of those who died or were wounded. You were the officer behind the barricade at the Bogside when one of the young marchers was wounded and one of his mates raised a white handkerchief so that he could render aid to the young man, you gave an order to shoot the man with the flag. Today, you are going to beg for mercy with a white flag."

They brought the naked Palmer outside in the chilly fog and walked him down his driveway toward the main road. They were about one hundred yards from his front door where his car was parked with his driver locked in the trunk. They removed his hand cuffs and gave him a white handkerchief.

He was given these instructions by one of the men, "You are to run to your front door and as you run I will use this revolver to shoot at you. I only have four bullets and as you start running, count to ten, then raise the flag. At that point, I will fire one shot at you. If I miss, you run again, count to ten, and raise your flag. I will fire at you again, and if you make it to your car before I shoot you, I will not pursue you any further. You have about thirty seconds to get your fat ass moving…Go! Go!"

As Palmer ran, or waddled, he raised the flag after about ten seconds. When the first shot was fired, it entered the back of Palmers head and he died instantly.

The man who fired the gun said, "Damn, I'm a better shot than I thought I was."

The two men entered a waiting car with three very large bags containing money that they thought was in excess of one million British pounds. It had been a great night and an *outstanding* morning.

FACT:

On "Bloody Sunday" in Derry, January 30, 1972, Patrick Joseph

Doherty, age thirty-one was shot from behind while attempting to crawl to safety in the forecourt of Rossville Flats.

Bernard McGuigan, age forty-one was shot in the back of the head when he went to help Patrick Doherty. McGuigan had been waving a white handkerchief at the soldiers to indicate his peaceful intentions.

****

George Barker, a former British Army officer, was one of the men in command of the 1st Battalion Parachute Regiment, some of the first troops ordered to fire upon the unarmed Catholic civil rights marchers at Bogside in Derry on "Bloody Sunday" in 1972. He was also very vocal about calling all the Irish "trash."

Mr. Barker owned a very lucrative real estate agency in London. On the 29th January, Barker received a phone call from someone who sounded American, making an inquiry about a twenty-sixth floor penthouse that Barker had for lease in the upscale Mayfair section of London. The gentleman was interested in a two year lease for his company.

George Barker thought to himself, "Why pay one of my employees commission when I can handle the showing myself?"

Barker made an appointment with the man who identified himself as Mr. Joseph Higgins. The two men agreed to meet the next day at the site.

On the 30th of January, at 10:00 a.m., Barker was greeted at his condo by two very well dressed men who both had American accents. The men introduced themselves as representatives of a company called "Vandalay Industries," which was located in New York City.

The man who was introduced as Mr. Higgins looked around the condo and admired the great view of London from the deck. Higgins suddenly turned and pointed a weapon at Mr. Barker and ordered him to sit at a table and pay very close attention to what he was about to say.

Higgins asked George Barker, "Do you know what today's date is?"

Barker looked at Higgins with a blank stare.

Higgins told Barker that it was the 30th of January and then asked Barker if he could reconstruct in his mind any connection to this date. George paused and said, "Jesus…Bloody Sunday."

Higgins then told Barker, "You're a lot smarter than you look."

Higgins then ordered Barker to sit and listen closely to what he was about to say.

"You have two granddaughters that attend the Green Street School in London. It is now 10:20 a.m. and they are both on the track team at their school. For the next thirty minutes, they will remain at the track training with about sixteen other girls. As they run around the oval track on one side, they are running south. I have a man in an adjacent building that overlooks the south side of the track who is armed with a hunting rifle that is equipped with a 200X Excel telescope. He can easily shoot the balls off of a fly at 400 yards. You sir can save the lives of both girls by writing a letter that I will dictate to you."

Barker started to stand up, but was pushed back into his seat by Higgins who gave him a stern warning, "Sit still listen and learn!"

The man who was with Higgins took out his cell phone, dialed a number, and asked whoever was on the other end if all was in order. The man repeated his conversation so Barker could hear every word.

"Both girls are on the track. They just removed their blue and gold warm up jackets and are in the process of running laps. He can take them both down in less than fifteen seconds."

The shooter was told to stay on the line.

Higgins then instructed Barker to start writing. Barker did as he was told.

Dear Family and Friends,

So many years after "Bloody Sunday" in Derry, I am still terribly disturbed about the events of that day. My feelings have been hidden well, but now on the anniversary of the massacre, I can take no more!

> *Please don't hate me because of this selfish act but*
> *I have no choice.*
> *I love you all…George.*

When Higgins read the letter, he knocked Barker to the floor and said, "You slimy son of a bitch, I think I will have someone go to Market Street and not only kill your wife but also your dog. Do you think we are stupid? You never sign 'George' to any personal correspondence. You always sign 'Georgie.' Do it one more time and do it right."

When the letter was finished, Barker was told to get a chair move it to the balcony. The man on the cell phone said that the girls were still on the track and everything was a go. At that point, the former British Army hero of Derry,

who had ordered the shooting of unarmed children was in tears. He was instructed to stand on the chair and jump or the girls would die.

Barker jumped.

Higgins, or as we know him as Francis X., and the other "cousin" Joe Wheaton took the stairs to the twenty-second floor. They put the plastic gun in a fast food bag, dumped it in a trash receptacle, and rode the elevator to the lobby. The entire area was in chaos.

Francis and Joe walked to an American coffee shop and began gloating about their encounter with George Barker. Francis said, "It's too bad the stupid bastard didn't know that the Green Street School is closed today and that the kids are all on a field trip to the Tower of London. I hope his granddaughters enjoyed the day"

Chapter 20

Back in Boston, Francis X. had received a few messages left by Michelle, inquiring about her brother Joseph. Francis called Michelle and told her that Joseph had left the boat in Prince Edward Island with thirty-eight thousand U.S. dollars, which he had deposited in a PEI bank. A week later, he withdrew the money and told his co-workers that he was headed for Montreal. Francis also told her that he had a close friend on the Royal Canadian Mounted Police. Francis said that he would contact him and ask for help in locating her brother.

Two days later, he called Michelle and told her that his friend Tom Kiley, the Canadian police officer discovered that Joseph had rented a car in Montreal, and along with a girl he met in PEI, drove from Montreal to Toronto. He said that Tom Kiley was going to continue checking on Joseph's location. Francis thought that Michelle was getting to be a real pain in the ass.

****

Natural gas is odorless and colorless. Suppliers put an odorant called mercaptan into the gas pipe systems that has its' own unique smell.

Francis asked a few of his people if they could get some mercaptan from the local gas company. He also told them if need be, he would send someone to Beaumont, Texas or Mobile, Alabama where the odorant was manufactured.

When asked why he needed such a thing, Francis replied, "I have a plan."

Francis X. met with Bill Moroney a few days later, and Bill told Francis that he had enough mercaptan to stink up the entire City of Boston. Francis instructed Moroney to go to Michelle's neighborhood and drop a little mercaptan into a couple of the storm drains near her house. He further instructed Moroney to go back the following week and do the same thing except on a different part of the street. Francis said that it will give the area a good healthy smell and would cause the gas company to go nuts trying to find a leak.

That night, Francis X. flew back to Ireland.

Chapter 21

The next day when Francis arrived in Ireland, he held a meeting at O'Donnell's Kells I in Dublin.

There are four O'Donnell's Pubs in Ireland. The Kells I and the Kells IV which are both in Dublin. The Kells II in Waterford, and the Kells III in Galway. They are all owned by W.D. O'Donnell.

There were fifteen people at his meeting which was held in a private room in the pub. At the meeting, Francis announced, "I have a plan." While Francis X. had the attention of his most trusted confidants, he knew it was time to reveal his plan. All of the work, all of the death, all of the pain, Francis X. had brought them together for one purpose and one purpose only; and that purpose was about to be told.

"Cousins, you have all done so well these past few months with the tasks I have assigned to you. I know none of you would ever question my motive, as you know I am looking out for your lives in the same way you look out for mine. I think, however, you should all be made aware of what your efforts have amounted to and I want you to envision the following scenario.

On New Year's Eve in New York City, people from all over the world gather to witness the famous ball drop on Times Square. That

81

'ball' is no ordinary mass object. It is one thousand pounds, six feet in diameter and it is made up of 504 individual pieces of Waterford Crystal...Irish pride. Do you think those American bastards thank the Irish for their ingenuity, or their hard hours of labor and their thankless positions for creating such a masterpiece for the world to behold? No! That, my friends, is the reason why Ireland will take the fame so rightly robbed from them. Of the 504 crystal panels, 72 of them get replaced every year. You will remember that Liam O'Reilly and Peter Clarke both work at Waterford Crystal and at this point, I am certain they will do anything we ask of them in order to seek vengeance on the people who have wronged them. They will take the 72 panels and dip them in 'FX's HELL.' Now, this will be no ordinary celebration. To mark the end of the war in the Middle East, the Americans are inviting several well known dignitaries from the United Kingdom to enjoy the festivities. Among them will be the Duke and Duchess of Gloucester, Prince and Princess Michael of Kent, and the Princess Alexandra, along with the American Secretary of State, the Speaker of the House and Madam President herself. This will teach the Americans and the English that they have screwed us over long enough. Now, I cannot tell you anymore about this plan. I can only tell you that I have a meeting with O'Reilly and Clarke in Waterford to let them know what is going on. You will all be called on to do various things and I ask that you keep as much faith in me as you have had in these past few months; perhaps even more. Now, is there anyone in here opposed to my plan?"

Francis observed the room. Not one hand.

****

In Waterford, the town was bustling with the festivities of the Christmas light ceremonies about to take place in a few days.

Inside O'Donnells Kells II, John Fahy, Liam O'Reilly, and Peter Clarke were sitting at the bar listening to Francis'plan. They felt a sense of national pride and personal responsibility to carry out his sinister plan and they could not agree more with the statements that Francis had made.

"This, gentleman, is not just for your families whose wounds may never heal. This is for every Irishman; your father, your grandfather and his grandfather who dealt with the adversities and undermining of being thought of as a second class citizen in a world where the Irish have given so much. They have contributed to the arts and culture and bettered the lives of millions without even so much as a thank you. No, this task isn't for the weak of heart. It is for the strong of heart; a heart that knows Ireland's pain and strife and wants her to grow forceful...no, invincible, in the eyes of the world. Gentleman, friends, are you with me?"

Peter and Liam's faces were fixated on Francis' eyes. Perhaps beneath the black coal of his gaze was fire because they could not have been more onboard.

Peter raised his glass.

"To Ireland. May we bring back her glory."

The men all raised their glasses.

"To Ireland!"

****

On the West coast of Ireland in Galway was O'Donnell's Kells III, which was managed by a man named Craig Loftus. There was one bouncer who worked there who was specifically hired by Francis X. He went by the name of C.C. Matthews. Francis' sister Kathleen and her partner, Mary, frequented the pub.

One night Kathleen and Mary were sitting in their normal booth when a man approached the table and started talking to Kathleen. He was a rowdy drunk who looked at the two women and drunkenly slurred, "You should be with a real man and not this queer bitch."

Kathleen then slapped him in the face and he slapped her back. She then sat back down and C.C. Matthews came over, took the man by the throat and shoved him up against the wall of the pub. He gritted through his teeth at the man.

"If you ever show your face around this pub, I'll have your head!" The man left in a huff. C.C. looked at Kathleen and noticed that her mouth was bleeding. He suggested that she call her brother. She reneged.

"You know how Francis is. I don't want him causing trouble."

Kathleen looked to Mary, who for the most part didn't care much for Francis, but said to Kathleen that any man who was coward enough to hit a woman deserved to deal with the likes of Francis. Kathleen then made the phone call to America and told Francis what had happened.

Francis said he would take care of it and nothing more was said.

A week later, the "Garda" discovered the brutally beaten body of a man by the name of George Pasley. He was castrated and tied to a tree in the middle of Eyre Square. The police were familiar with him since they had dealt with him on more than one occasion. Pasley would sit on the board walk on Salt Hill beach ogling girls and women and would sometimes make crude remarks towards them. Pasley was thought of as a pervert. Although the police were investigating his death, one could be assured that it was not a very high priority case. They felt he must have angered someone's wife, mother, daughter or sister.

Chapter 22

Francis returned stateside and was told that the gas company had received numerous phone calls about the gas odors emanating from the area around Michelle's house. Hugh Griffin, a worker from the gas company, told Francis that they would attempt to track the leaks using a "sniffer" which detects any natural gas in the air. The "sniffer" takes samples of the air which go through a flame ionization machine which will show any combustible particles in the air.

Francis knew that this was going to be a very interesting few days and he dispatched Bill Moroney back to the Woburn neighborhood to spread a little more mercaptan around the city streets.

When Francis found out that Moroney was finished with the task at hand, he picked up the phone and called Michelle for a rendezvous at their favorite bar.

The date was going seemingly perfect until Michelle stopped eating and started to cry. Francis was mildly taken aback from this display of emotion and asked her what the issue might be.

Michelle responded, "I'm just really worried about my brother. With my mother in a nursing home and you always back and forth between countries, I am just feeling really alone right now."

Francis took her hand and kissed it softly. "Darling, you know that as long as you know me you will never be alone. As far as your brother is concerned, call me crazy but I have a feeling that the two of you will be together very soon."

Michelle smiled. How could she not? Francis always seemed to know what to say and always made her feel calm when he spoke.

They returned to Francis' condo for the evening. Little did she know what was taking place in her home while she was sleeping.

A confidante of Francis used the key Michelle so trustingly gave him to enter her home. With the use of specially designed tools, the intruder went into Michelle's living room and carefully cracked the glass of the light bulbs in the lamps on her two end tables. She did so with great care so not to rupture the filament. After that it was on to the kitchen where the intruder loosened a flex hose in the back of Michelle's stove, which allowed a very small amount of gas to escape.

For the record, it takes 84 parts gas and 16 parts oxygen to create a volatile explosive.

Michelle was relaxed and optimistic when she arrived home to an empty house. She noticed the faint smell of gas in the air but thought nothing more of it since she had noticed the smell for quite some time. She then walked into her hallway and flicked on the light switch. The explosion was so great that it damaged the four surrounding houses. Nothing was left standing in her house that was taller than a refrigerator and fireplace.

****

The next day was Sunday and, as Francis was leaving Mass in the North End of Boston, he picked up the Sunday Globe to read about the terrible fire that left one person dead in Woburn. The explosion was suspected to be caused by a gas leak. Michelle Patrick was the only victim named.

A few days later, Michelle's funeral was held in Cambridge and she was laid to rest in the plot where her father was buried. Francis and several of his "Cousins" attended the service.

At the cemetery as people began to walk away, Francis went over to the gravesite, made the sign of the cross, and dropped a single rose on the grave. He looked over to one of his friends and said, "Remind me to make a donation to the Sister's of Saint Joseph in honor of Michelle when we get home."

One of his friends retorted, "Jesus Francis, you're so generous and caring. You ought to button up your shirt…your heart's popping out!"

The men laughed.

Francis then said solemnly, "Well, I did her a favor. She wanted to be with her brother and I'd say right about now that's exactly where she is."

****

The day after the funeral, Francis X. met with a group of his people in Boston and gave them some information about his plans for New Year's Eve. He asked if anyone had any questions.

One girl asked Francis why he wanted to rid the world of the Yanks and Brits?

"Well," Francis said, "let me explain why I have such strong feelings about both of the groups that you just mentioned. You all know what happened on 'Bloody Sunday.' But it goes back a lot further than that. Michelle and I spoke often about civil rights and she would remind me of the four hundred years of slavery her people had endured. I told her that in the 1600s, the blacks were brought to colonies and to islands called the 'Sugar Islands.'

About the same, between 1649 and 1657, was a time called 'the heyday of Irish slave trade,' where the Irish had as many people in servitude on the islands and in America as the blacks did, thanks to Lord Cromwell.

In Septmeber of 1653, a ship called 'The Goodfellow' arrived in Boston Harbor carrying 550 Irish captives. When Cromwell's army crushed a revolt above the River Shannon, thousands of Irish soldiers fled to France and Spain. Their wives and children were hunted down and sold as servants in the American Colonies and the West Indies. The Goodfellow's master, paraded a select group of children on deck for inspection by the citizens of Boston who flocked to buy the Irish boys and girls. They were to be bound as servants for at least ten years. Some of the slaves were as young as nine years old.

During the civil war, as ships arrived from Ireland in New York Harbor, many Irish men were told that if they wanted to stay in the country they must join the army and had to do so right then and there on the docks.

Yes, I told Michelle that black people were suppressed, but so were the Irish. Not only were they forced to join the army, but the only civilian jobs they could get were the ones that had the highest percentage of disease and death.

America's highest award for valor is the 'Medal of Honor.' More men from Ireland and men of Irish decent have been awarded the medal, more than by any other nationality. Some have been awarded it twice.

In Boston, there were many signs that could be seen hanging in all different places saying 'Help Wanted,' and 'NO IRISH NEED APPLY.' Some say that all the unions were controlled by the Irish and that was the reason for the signs, but I still think that religion had a lot to do with it.

If you notice today, you can't use the 'N' word when talking about a black person. That's obviously great and shows that the black community has made great strides to help stamp out discrimination. How about the Irish? They still have a police van that picks up drunks or others headed for jail. What is that van called? The 'Paddy Wagon.' How about we call it the 'Guinea' wagon or the 'Pollack' wagon or the 'Nigger' wagon? It's still called the 'Paddy Wagon' after all of us Irish drunks. Where are the civil rights people now?

Do I have an axe to grind? Maybe I do. They shipped my father back to Ireland from America to be killed by the British. Does anyone disagree?" No one did.

One of the cousins asked Francis X. how hard it was to actually kill another person. Francis said that was a really tough question but, like Jesus did in the Bible, he would answer the question with a story.

"When I graduated from college and was a newly commissioned second lieutenant, myself and two other graduates were having a mini celebration in an Irish bar on State Street in Boston. We were a bit noisy and attracted some attention. The waiter brought us a round of drinks and said it was from a man at the bar. We said thanks and then invited the man to join us. He turned out to be a retired First Sergeant in the U.S. Army. We chatted and had a few more rounds. He asked what career field we were interested in pursuing, and I told him I was looking into being part of the U.S. Special Forces.

The man said that he thought a 'green beret' would fit just fine on my square Irish head. He then asked me how I would feel about killing someone.

I told him I never thought about it and asked him if he had ever killed anyone. He told us he once killed a man in an accident with an army truck. It was not his fault so he never felt bad about it. After all it was an accident. He then related a story that kept us all on the edge of our chairs.

During the cold war, he and another soldier were on the border between East and West Germany, and Czechoslovakia. Their unit was temporarily located about ten kilometers from the border. They had a jeep and went riding around, and as we say in the army, 'just goofing off.' They parked their vehicle, chain locked it, and then began walking around the edge of a farm. He said that they weren't sure of their exact position, but they knew that the border was near although there were no border guard towers in sight. They had neither seen nor heard anyone during the walk around the area, however, when they started back to retrieve the jeep, they could see three figures heading in their direction. At that point, they didn't know if they had wandered over the border or if they were still on the West German side. They both knew that they were in a bad situation.

The retired First Sergeant further related that he unlocked his weapon and told the other soldier, whose name was Mitch, to unlock his. The First Sergeant said he had a .45 caliber grease gun and his partner had a .30 caliber carbine.

As the three men approached, both he and Mitch could see that they were border guards, most likely Czech. They looked anything but friendly. They attempted to speak with the three guards; however, the guards did not understand English and both he and Mitch could not understand them.

The three guards angrily faced them and continued talking. The guard on the right then started moving slowly to his left as the two others began moving to the right. The First Sergeant said that it looked like the guards were trying to flank him and Mitch.

At that moment, the guy on the right said something and was about to move his weapon from his side to his front and that's when the First Sergeant told us that he shot him. He said he put one in the guard's chest and the other two in his face.

At the same time, Mitch shot the other two. As the one on the right went down, the First Sergeant turned and emptied his magazine into the other two, although he was sure that they were both dead.

After the shooting, neither man could hear a sound. The First Sergeant said, "

'It was almost eerie.' He then went on to say, 'We collected all the brass, scuffed up what few footprints we had made and walked back to our vehicle. After the ride back to our unit, we expected all hell to break loose but nothing happened.'

The First Sergeant further related the following:

Ten days after the incident, they returned to their home station which was about seventy miles from the border. They hadn't seen any news accounts about the shooting nor heard anything about any investigations.

The First Sergeant and Mitch spoke about the incident and how they felt. He said that neither of them had any flash backs, loss of sleep, or bad dreams. It didn't seem to have any effect on either of them, except for one thing.

Every time the ex-militant, First Sergeant heard the national anthem playing when he was a young soldier, he would get butterflies in his stomach. It was a great feeling. He said that after the shooting of the guards, he seemed to get the same butterfly like feeling whenever he thought about killing them. It was then he knew that he was in the right profession.

The First Sergeant then related his thought about shooting people, which is to follow the golden rule. 'Do it to them before they do it to you.'

Francis X. then said it had been a great night and that he really enjoyed talking with the old soldier."

Someone asked Francis about his first encounter with death in combat. Francis said that it was up close and personal and he did it with a knife. He also said that he had butterflies for a while. He said, "I guess that First Sergeant and I have more in common than our first names."

Chapter 23

Francis told Clarke that he'd never gone to the Waterford Chrystal Factory, and he decided to take a tour.

Francis was very impressed with the history of the Waterford Chrystal Factory. It was started in 1783 by two brothers. To the present day, all of the master cutters make their own designs by hand. There are no computers, no robots; just pure Irish labor. The master cutters have made golf trophies, tennis trophies and even Super Bowl trophies. When you walk into the display room, it looks like an ice palace.

Clarke and O'Reilly worked alone at the factory with no supervision, which would make it easy for them to paint the panels of the New Year's Eve Ball with "FX's Hell."

Francis was impressed with the operation. He had about a month before New Year's Eve in Times Square to implement his plan. He needed to meet with Clarke and O'Reilly to discuss their duties.

Francis decided to invite them to one of O'Donnell's Kells II's famous "Hooley Nights." There was dancing and live music and their families and friends were welcomed with open arms. Francis pulled the two gentlemen into the back room and asked them how the progress at the factory was going.

Both O'Reilly and Clarke said that the panels were completed and had been shipped en route to America.

Francis was pleased and told the men there would be two great surprises for each of them: one which lay in New York City and the other was 100,000 Euros upon their return to Ireland.

They declined the offer.

O'Reilly spoke.

"Francis, you are too kind but we are true Irish. The revenge we have for our families is payment enough. We work honestly and do not wish to be compensated as such. Your offer is far too much."

Francis insisted saying that he wanted to insure that the two men had enough money to take care of their families in these troubled times. He also offered them a fishing trip to Florida after their trip to New York.

The three men toasted with glasses of Paddy's Irish Whiskey and went about the party.

Before the men left, Francis said, "I saw Johnny O'Feeley out there. Would you please let him know I wish to speak with him in the back room?"

O'Feeley, who came from a well known, and at one time, a very well respected family from Galway, met with Francis in the backroom. His brother was a professor at a university just outside of Boston. His father was a surgeon who lost his license to practice and served three years in jail for performing illegal abortions, among other unlawful acts. He was also the doctor who performed the botched abortion on Kayleigh Clarke. It may have appeared to be a botched abortion, but in fact it was the perfect homicide!

Mr. O'Feeley was somewhat of an electronic genius. He was responsible for Ireland having the computer capabilities to host many of the world's mobile phone companies on the Irish shores. He was one of the brightest minds to ever come out of Ireland and he was indebted to Francis for a number of favors.

It was finally time for Francis to request them.

Johnny was going to travel to New York City on 31st of December to program a remote control that would be able to set off "FX's Hell" from a hotel window, just far enough away from Times Square. It was a massive undertaking, as the radio waves needed to be magnified, only enough to perform the task, but not to be picked up by any of the security in the area.

O'Feeley said he needed to reach out to Michael McGrath from the Galway office so the two of them could work together. He swore that McGrath would be as loyal to Francis as he was.

Francis agreed.

Two days later, Francis was called by O'Feeley and McGrath for a demonstration. They had a small plastic box, a cell phone, and cheesy grins on their faces. Francis was intrigued to say the least. They headed to a farm on the outskirts of Rathfarnham County Dublin.

The two men laced a tree with "FX's Hell" and returned with Francis to his car, which was parked over a mile away. Once they were in the car, O'Feeley took out the cell phone and dialed a number as though he were ordering take away. Suddenly, the tree blew up and split right in half. They then went back and put more of "FX's Hell" on the tree and drove away from the farm. They went into town and were sitting at O'Donnell's Kells I having a pint when O'Feeley pulled out his mobile phone and dialed the number again. They later returned to the farm to find that tree had completely melted and was destroyed.

They explained to Francis that from Dublin to New York, the cell phone connection would take approximately fourteen seconds to detonate "FX's Hell" on the Times Square ball.

Francis was thrilled. He instructed them to go to New York City and scout out a hotel near Times Square, as there was not much time before New Year's Eve.

O'Feeley and McGrath were delighted to get away on the company expenses and left for America straight away.

****

Francis met Dolores Dargin, the manager of O'Donnell's Kells IV, in the Ballsbridge area of Dublin, where he instructed Dolores to close the bar to the public on New Year's Eve in order to have a private function for his employees.

Dolores said that she was happy to host such an occasion.

Francis had memos sent out to his offices in both America and Ireland. The managers of all of the O'Donnell's Kells bars were invited as well as certain employees. They would hire temporary staff to work on that night to replace the employees who were invited to the party.

At the Kells IV, after his meeting with Dolores, Francis X. was sitting with several friends, when Devlin McFay asked Francis, "Did you forsake your mother's land? Why do you spend so much time in America?"

Francis was never one to decline and opportunity to tell his story, so he sat on a wooden stool and looked into the eyes of his friends. His speech was a bit slurred, but clear enough to hear his soul.

Francis explained, "I went into that hell hole for a reason. I went on my own free will and accord. I learned everything a man should need to know in life and more. I learned how to make bombs, kill people and got paid to kill people, all while receiving the best training in the world. Over there, they called it Bush's War, but I didn't call it that. A war is a war. We would have to call World War II, Roosevelt's War or Vietnam, Kennedy's War or the Korean War, Truman's War. Blame it on anyone you want, it's still a war. People die. I have no love for the Americans and their bloodlust because I think they speak when not spoken too and when they do speak, they don't say enough.

Take the Middle East for example, I would make it into one giant parking lot. Gone, the whole lot of them! It wouldn't solve it all but it sure would stop a whole hell of a lot. That's what they should do."

Francis had tears in his eyes from the passion in which he delivered his speech. Dolores chimed in, "My Francis, you are as sensitive as ever, aren't you?"

She and Francis then left the party together. Many of the people in the room thought that Dolores and Francis had more than professional relationships going on and theirs was surely more.

****

Over in New York City, O'Feeley and McGrath were checking out Times Square, Broadway and 42nd Street in Midtown Manhattan.

To the two Irishmen who had never ventured outside of the Emerald Isle, Manhattan was like an electric planet full of aliens. People, places, sounds, smells, feelings and fears all ran about this tiny island with no one taking any extra notice to the amazement that surrounded them.

The two found some bars, enjoyed some nightlife and the evening's festivities. While in Times Square's famous "Pig 'N' Whistle" pub, the men ran into a married couple originally from Ireland. The woman's maiden name was Hession and her married name was Coffee. They were from Roscommon and the four bonded quickly over life across the sea. The woman took a liking to her fellow Irishmen. She worked for a very well known hotel in Times Square and was not only able to get them reservations for the 31st of December, but she was able to get them a family and friends rate.

Francis talked with O'Feeley and McGrath and was glad to hear things were coming together.

The day after Christmas, Dolores and Francis returned to Boston to meet with his staff there. Francis explained to them that he had not forgotten about their Christmas bonuses and that they were to attend a party in Dublin on New Year's Eve where all of their hard work would be rewarded amply. He was excited to see their faces light up. Francis made only one request of his employees; they were not allowed to bring guests to the party.

"We have no need for strangers on what is sure to be a great evening for all," Francis said and they all agreed.

The next day, Francis took the Amtrak down to New York City to check out the progress of his two key players, O'Reilly and Clarke. When he saw the work on the New Year's Eve ball was complete, he expressed his gratitude to the two men.

"Gentleman, you have gone above and beyond what was expected and I want to reward you as such. As promised, tomorrow the two of you will be taken on an all expenses paid trip to Florida. There, you will be able to enjoy the fruits of your labor with all the food, booze and fishing you can want for a few days. You have earned your rest. I want you back home for New Year's Eve though."

Francis told them to check out of the hotel the next day around

10 a.m. There would be a car waiting to take them to JFK airport for their flight to Fort Lauderdale, Florida.

Upon arriving in Florida, outside the terminal, a car and driver would pick them up and drive them to one of the best hotels on Fort Lauderdale Beach.

****

The two Irishmen had never seen such a grand hotel with all the amenities. Their suite had a full bar, two bedrooms, a Jacuzzi, and a view of the beach that had them mesmerized for over an hour. Clarke had been to Spain once but it could not compare to Florida. They thought they were in heaven.

The next morning, the two men were picked up and driven to the marina to meet the crew and board the fishing boat. It was a magnificent Sea Ray, fifty-five feet long. The name of the fine vessel was the "SEAKER III."

Both O'Reilly and Clarke thought the three members of the crew were comedians who were hired to entertain them on the trip. First, they all claimed to be the captain of the boat. There were two named Gerry and one named Rob. The first captain was tall Gerry with glasses and a funny hair cut (it looked like his wife must've cut it). The second captain was bearded Gerry and the third was Rob with a weird sense of humor. They were all called "captain."

They left Fort Lauderdale that morning and headed east toward the Bahamas.

The following day around 10 a.m., the "SEAKER III" arrived back at the marina. They had their share of fish but the only people on the boat were the three "captains." After securing the boat, they took a plane to Boston that night.

Two nights before New Year's Eve, the three "captains" were in an upscale hotel overlooking the Boston Common, and having dinner with Kathleen O'Donnell. She was interested in their latest fishing trip. They told her it went well, but they returned to port with less gear. She asked what they meant by less gear.

Captain Gerry (the tall one) explained that it took 200 pounds of anchor chain for each of the two objects they had to sink plus two ounces of lead.

Kathleen asked what the lead was used for, and Captain Gerry explained that they had put lead in the fishermen's ears.

She wanted to know how they managed that, and Captain Rob (with the weird sense of humor) said, "With a .38 Caliber Chief's Special."

The three "captains" told Kathleen that if she ever needed someone to feed the crabs in South Florida again, that they would always be available.

They wished her a happy New Year and she wished them the same. She handed each of them a thick envelope and, the next day, Kathleen was on a plane back to Ireland.

****

On New Year's Eve day, O'Feeley was back at the hotel in New York City overlooking Times Square. He had all his electronic gadgets that were needed to put "FX's Hell" into play for the big celebration.

On a small table near the window, he had a line of sight right into the giant crystal ball. With two alligator clips, he attached the cell phone box containing the radio beam transmitter. Everything looked fine. O'Feeley waved goodbye to the big ball and exited the hotel. He then flagged down a cab to the airport for his trip back to Ireland for the New Year's Eve party.

Chapter 24

Back in Dublin, all the plans were in place for the big celebration. New Year's in Ireland would be celebrated five hours earlier than in New York.

At the Kells IV, where the private party was being held for Francis X.'s special employees, Dolores, the manager, McGrath and Francis were in the pub office having a New Year's drink.

Francis toasted, "To two Happy New Year's; one here and one in America." The three toasted and decided to go back to the party. Francis asked Dolores

who had keys to the office. She said she that she had the only one. Francis then asked McGrath if everything was in order. McGrath assured him it was.

Around 11:30 p.m. Francis gave a little speech to the guests, thanking them for their loyalty and reminded them that later on that night they would receive the profit sharing checks.

"I also have another surprise for all of you. For years, you have all thought of me as the brains behind our company and I am always treated as the boss. Now, I want to introduce to you the person who is responsible for our entire operation; our Chief Executive Officer and the owner of our pub's travel agency and our real estate companies.

Please raise your glasses and join me in toasting W.D. O'Donnell. She is Kathleen's and my mother, the beautiful Winifred Doherty O'Donnell."

Winifred Doherty O'Donnell was born on a farm just north of Milford, County Donegal Ireland. She was the middle child in a family of nine. The Doherty family were Roman Catholic, hard working farmers.

From early childhood, Winifred exhibited more than just average intelligence. In school, she was far more advanced than others her age. At the age of sixteen, Winifred received a full scholarship from her church to attend the University of Dublin.

As a child, Winifred would sit with the family and listen to stories told by her father and grandmother about the difficult times Ireland had with the British. They were stories about brutality, slavery, torture and the killing of the Irish Catholics and the destruction of the Catholic churches throughout Ireland. Winifred spent many a night reading by the light of the fireplace until the wee hours. Her favorite books were on Irish and American History.

Upon graduation from the University of Dublin with a degree in business, she moved to America to further her education with a Masters in Business from Harvard University.

She returned to Ireland and had been an executive for an American company working in Dublin; however, her life was changed forever when she met Bernard, "Barney" O'Donnell, a full time construction supervisor and part time Irish terrorist with a deep hatred of all things British. Winifred shared all of his feelings about the "Brits." They married, had two children and the rest is history.

After Barney's murder, Winifred, a very savvy business person, worked very hard to become one of the wealthiest women in Ireland and Boston. She also became one of the most dangerous women in the whole world.

With her family, Francis X. and Kathleen, she owned many successful businesses. They bought a large sea resort frequented by many Irish on the coast of Spain. Winifred stayed in Spain for nine weeks and upon her return to Ireland; her Spanish was flawless. She kept a low profile and was a true lady at all times. She did let her feelings be known at times, such as her statements about the "Brits" to some of her friends. She had been heard to say, "England is another evil empire full of uptight gin drinking, lying whore masters."

A cheer went up and there were more than one gasps of surprise as Mrs. O'Donnell entered the room. She had Asian features, high cheek bones, black as coal eyes, and a smile that could have melted a glacier.

She stood between her daughter Kathleen, and son Francis X. and spoke to the group. She thanked them for all the years of loyalty and hard work and hoped for even better years ahead.

Mrs. O'Donnell mingled with the folks and managed to speak one on one with almost every person in the room.

Francis addressed the group one more time and told him that his sister and mother had to leave to attend another function. He asked everyone if they left to please be back around 4:15 a.m. or 4:30 a.m. as Kathleen would return with their bonus checks and he wanted them all to see the ball drop on Times Square at 5a.m. He said the fireworks display would prove to be spectacular.

Francis, Kathleen, and W.D. O'Donnell left for Dalky. Other chosen personnel slipped out one at a time and also proceeded to Dalky. Those who remained could not believe that the big boss was none other than the mother of Francis X. and Kathleen. They thought this was the biggest surprise of the evening. But there was a lot to come.

At home in Dalky, the O'Donnells were surrounded with the folks they most trusted with their lives and those who also trusted the O'Donnell's with theirs.

There were about eighteen people in the house with the family while Francis addressed the group and said, "For years, I have been telling all of you when you speak always speak as if you are being videotaped and recorded because most of the time you are. Some people in the organization had not heeded this warning."

He told them that security was one of the most important factors in their business. He said that the house they were in was worth close to three million Euros and the one in Boston was worth two million dollars. What made them so expensive? It was that they had close to a million Euros worth of electronic security, and an electric shield around both houses to protect the family from ease droppers. They also de-bug the houses daily. Their electronic security system was equal to the CIA's or MI 6, or even better.

Francis went on to say, "Most of you are aware that we have a new team of employees joining us and they should be on board by February or March. There are twenty-seven in training. Ten in Texas, nine in New Mexico, and eight in Syria. We have four Americans and twenty-three Irish, all from Donegal, including six females. As you know, when they complete the required travel agent course, they will be proficient in the use of firearms, explosives, and numerous other things." Francis got a big laugh from the folks and all resumed to party.

Around 4:30 a.m., Francis X. walked into his office retrieved a cell phone, dialed a number and pushed send. Ten seconds later he returned the phone to his desk and joined the other guests.

They were all watching a live feed from Times Square when the show was suddenly interrupted with a news flash that here had been an explosion in Dublin, in the area called Ballsbridge. It was said that it "rocked the city" and updates would follow.

Needless to say no one in that house in Dalky was the least bit surprised when they heard about the blast in Ballsbridge. They knew damn right well what had happened.

A loud announcement then came over the TV saying that the explosion had destroyed a pub called O'Donnell's Kells IV and the reporter said, "Windows have been broken for over a half mile and six other buildings have sustained severe damage. The loss of life is not known at this time."

They changed channels and were watching the feed from America. They watched the ball in Times Square as the count down to the New Year started. Francis picked up a cell phone as the count went on…ten…nine…eight. At that point, Francis X. pushed send on the cell phone and the count went to four…three…two…one. All of Times Square erupted with cheer of "Happy New Year!"

Again, Francis dialed the number and again nothing happened

in Times Square. The entire crew at the house were in shock. They could not believe that

"FX's Hell" did not work.

With dawn came the scene of the Ballsbridge explosion on all the TV stations in Dublin. Two buildings had been completely destroyed. They still had not determined how many lives had been lost. A spokesperson for the O'Donnell family stated that a private party was being held at the pub for their employees at the time of the blast. Mr. O'Donnell and his sister were on their way to Ballsbridge. They also stated they would speak to the press later that week.

Francis and his electronic experts were trying to get a handle on what could have gone wrong in Times Square. O'Feeley explained how everything was assembled and they could not understand why it had failed.

Francis told them he had contacted a cousin, Red Ryan, who was the owner of a bar in Jersey City called the 2x2 Bar. He said Red was on his way to the hotel in Times Square to retrieve the phone and the other electronic equipment. O'Feeley said the thing looked like a cell phone with an answering machine. It would have been destroyed if the plan was successful.

About three hours later, Francis received a call from Red in America. Red told Francis that he had removed and destroyed all the equipment from the room in the hotel in Times Square. He also told Francis that when he examined everything before removing it, he found that one of the alligator clips had been disconnected from the cell phone.

After some discussion, Francis and the others figured the cell phone could have been jarred or moved by one of the hotel maids. At least now they had a reason why the device failed on New Year's Eve.

Two days later, the O'Donnell Family issued a statement. They said they had sadly lost thirty-one employees in the tragic explosion on New Years. Eight others in the surrounding area were killed and eleven injured. They announced that all the O'Donnell's business offices and pubs would be closed for thirty days in memory of those who lost their lives.

Six weeks after the great explosion, the authorities still had not determined the cause. The O'Donnell family did not want to rebuild the pub that they had lost. They made a request to the city to allow them to create a memorial park on the location for all who were killed that night. Their plans included flower beds and walkways lined with stones inscribed with the names of the deceased. It would be built and maintained by the O'Donnell Family. One city official said that they were the most caring and thoughtful family the city had ever seen.

In Waterford, O'Reilly and Clarke's disappearance was still a mystery. The last that anyone had heard from the two men was that they were in New York working on the New Year's Eve ball.

One Tuesday morning, two packages were delivered; one to the O'Reilly house and one to the Clarke House. When they opened the packages, similar notes were found that read: "Dear Widow Clarke" and "Dear Widow O'Reilly." It continued, "We hope this will help with the loss of your husband. Our sympathy." The notes were unsigned. In each box were bundles of one hundred Euros, amounting to one hundred thousand Euros in each. They had return addresses from a fake address in Galway City.

Francis X, his sister Kathleen and their mother Winifred Doherty O'Donnell were sitting in the Boston condo talking about the past and the future. They were all still disappointed with the outcome of the New York plan.

As they looked back on the latest events, Francis commented that he had warned all those killed in Dublin many times that they may be being videotaped or recorded; and they were. The people killed in the explosion were in the middle of a plan to take over the O'Donnell's business. There plan was a simple one.

The O'Donnell companies had planned a holiday for all the employees and their families at the company holiday villa on the coast of Spain. The trip was to take place at the end of February. They would have traveled in two planes, one morning flight and one afternoon flight. The person in charge of setting the trip was Ms. Josephine Kelly Lopes.

"Jo" Lopes was very instrumental in the plans to take over the

O'Donnell's business. The arrangements for the travel was to send two planes; the first plane in the morning with all the O'Donnell family and their close loyal friends, or as Francis referred to them as the "Cousins." This plane would be set to explode somewhere over the ocean, making the takeover very simple.

Francis made sure that all of the people involved with the takeover plan were in the pub on New Year's Eve, all thirty-one of them. He said the eight others that had died that night were collateral damage.

Francis then told his mother and sister that when you look at the whole picture and the plan, it works out to be a case of the old saying,

"Do it to them before they do it to you."

Winifred, their mother said, "You know, Waterford Crystal will be closed before this year is out."

Kathleen remarked, "How sad after hundreds of years."

Francis said, "That means the ball in Times Square will remain the same for the next New Year's Eve gala and they won't be changing panels."

"That's right," his mother replied.

Francis looked at them both and said, "I have a plan. Let's look back and see why thirty-one of our closest people had to die in Dublin on New Year's Eve. They were all very loyal people until one element changed their lives and that element was DRUGS. We know that we had a problem, no *they* had a problem that caused us to have a problem.

While many nations have had a losing war on drugs, a war that never ends, I think we, the O'Donnells should start our own war on drugs. We have been very careful in our operations around the world that's why the law enforcement community has never taken a second look at us. Most of the drugs originate in Central and South America.

In the Town of Weston, Massachusetts they have a delayed vocations seminary and with my educational background I could be ordained as a priest in about a year. If I were to accomplish this and become a missionary and volunteer my services to the drug producing countries, I could travel at will trying to save souls and help send those drug dealing bastards on a one way ticket to hell. Father Francis X. sounds good to me…and that's a plan."

ACKNOWLEDGEMENTS

To my wife Jean who had to live for the past few years with papers in every corner of the house, along with my calm attitude while writing this book.

To my son Danny and Gerry Izzi, M.D. They pushed until I finally put my thoughts on paper.

To my son Donald and Granddaughter Kerri...both spent hour after hour on the computer trying to put my thoughts into something that made sense.

To my right hand while putting this book together...my Grandson Sean. He managed to translate my recorded gibberish, "Pig Latin" and other strange words into English, to the point where it could be understood by normal people. ***Without Sean...I would still be on page one!***

To my son David for his constructive criticism which made me change some of the things in the book for the better.

To my son Kenneth...the major designer of the great book cover.

To Bernie Doherty, Beverly Sullivan, Joan Donnelly and Ashley DiSipio who made life easier by reading a rough copy and picking out the spelling and grammatical errors.

To the last but not least...my coffee drinking buddy Gerry Feeley who encouraged me weekly to keep the book moving. I would say he kept my morale up!

Again...Thank you all!!